Youngsters

By

Craig McCabe

All the best
Craig
x

Craig McCabe has asserted his right under the Copyright, Designs and Patents Act, 1988 to be identified as the author of this work.

First published by Trend 2008

All the characters in this book have no existence outside the imagination of the author, and have no relation whatsoever to anyone bearing the same name or names. They are not known or unknown individuals to the author, and all the incidents are pure invention.

Authors note –

After completing my first novel 'Driving Nowhere' I did not have many ideas for plots, so to continue my new found interest in writing, I decided to do an alternative take on one of my all-time favourite films, Young Guns. I wrote the story in the timeline of the late eighties, when I would have been around the same age as the boys in my story and coincidently, when the film was released.

One of the things I always have trouble with when I start writing are names for my characters, and even when Youngsters was completed and published, I was still not satisfied with it. The idea to change the names came at a point in my life when several of my childhood friends had passed away.

When we were young, we were often asked what we wanted to be when we grew up, but as a young teenager, neither of us knew what we wanted to do from one day to the next. They were innocent times, and as we grew older, we went down our separate paths, good and bad. Sometimes our paths crossed over and all those memories we had growing up came flooding back to us, and although we always had that connection to our past, we knew nothing was ever going to bring those moments back.

Partly, I wanted to change the names in tribute to those lost friends, but another part I would say they were changed because those are the names that should have been.

Craig Xx

Chapter 1

Mikey was only four when his parents were killed. They had been driving home during a bad winter when a lorry lost control due to black ice and hit them head on, killing them instantly. Mikey's only other family was Billy, his older brother. Billy had wanted to take care of Mikey and become his legal guardian but due to his age, and the fact that he had led a life of crime since he was a young boy, knew this would not be possible. Billy approached Charlie and Anna, an older couple who were friends of his parents and asked if they would foster Mikey. They had never had any children of their own and Billy knew they would give Mikey anything he needed. They lived in a large house in Bridgefoot, a small village only a mile north of Dundee. Occasionally, Billy would come to visit and Charlie would always try and persuade him to stay. Charlie knew Billy was in a lot of trouble and that it was only a matter of time before the authorities caught up with him, so when Billy made his excuses to leave, Charlie never pushed it.

The last time Mikey saw his brother was when he turned up at Charlie's late one night with a hold-all full of his belongings. Mikey remembers Billy giving him a hug and telling him that he was going away for a while but he would be in touch as often as he could. It was around this time that the police would come by looking for Billy. Charlie never gave them any information. After a few raised voices, Charlie would slam the door in their faces. Sometime after this, Mikey received a letter from Billy that had been stamped in a country that he couldn't pronounce. This went on for many years, as each letter he received would be posted from a different country. Mikey loved reading about Billy's adventures and every once in a while Billy would stay long enough in the same place for Mikey to write back. At school Mikey found it hard to bond with the other children as he was far superior both physically and mentally for his age. Mikey had learned so much about life from Charlie who was always willing to pass on his knowledge and advice, he was like the son he never had. Mikey lived with Charlie and Anna for six years, until, not long after his tenth birthday, Charlie had a heart attack and passed away. This was the moment when his whole life crumbled for a second time. The authorities in all their worldly wisdom had decided that Anna, due to her age was not capable of looking after a ten year old boy on her own and decided to move him on to another foster home.

    Within days of moving in with his new foster parents, Mikey learned with a harsh reality that nothing was ever going to be the same again. The loving, caring, secure environment he had grown to appreciate disappeared with a slap across the face as punishment for leaving his school bag lying on the floor in the hallway. Mikey did not cry like most ten year old boys would do when a fifteen stone grown man floored them. He did not even make a sound. He stood up, put his hand to his swollen face and stared back in shocked silence. As a ten year old boy who had been involved in many fights at school, he was more than capable of taking punches from other boys that were two, sometimes three years his senior, and although Charlie had taught him many ways to defend himself, he knew he had no chance against a grown man who was twice his size and weight. That first slap was the start of a two year struggle against physical abuse that he had to endure from Harry, his new foster father. There was never any verbal abuse from Harry, that all came from Linda his foster mother. Each time he heard her ranting and raving at Harry, he knew what was coming. It wasn't long after that first slap that the beatings really started. Mikey would try his best to fight back but each time he stood up to Harry, the beatings became more severe. Harry wasn't stupid though, he hardly ever hit Mikey where it would show. The back of the head was his favourite and sometimes when Mikey stood his ground, the stick would come out, but this was only used on Mikey's legs, the lower the better as these would be explained as football injuries.

    During these two years Mikey ran away many times. He had a social worker assigned to his case and Mikey told him on many occasions that he was being abused and had actually shown the bruises that he endured by one of his beatings from Harry. This was all to no avail, as Harry quickly dismissed them as bruises from Mikey fighting at school. It was also during this time that Mikey lost contact with Billy. He still sent letters to Anna and she would repost them to Mikey's new address but he never received them. Each time Mikey ran away he made his way to Anna's house, but the police knew where he was heading and would be sitting waiting on him when he arrived.

Two years later, Anna, due to her lack of mobility, had been moved into a residential home and Mikey was never informed. He ran away once again and was found sitting on the door-step of the boarded up home. He was returned once more to his foster parents, where, as usual, they would create a whiter than white environment for the benefit of the social workers and police. It was agreed by all parties that for Mikey's own benefit and for Anna's health, that he would not be given her new address. As soon the social workers and police were out of sight, Mikey knew what was coming. He shook with fear as Harry sat opposite him with his evil stare waiting on Linda to finish her tirade of abuse. She went on and on at how they took him in when he had no-one and this was how he repaid them by bringing the police to her door. It was time for Harry to teach him a lesson he would never forget. Mikey was sent to his room. He sat on the edge of his bed and tried to prepare himself mentally for what was to come. He could hear them downstairs arguing and then the sound of heavy footsteps. He couldn't take it any longer. Knowing now that he didn't have anywhere to run away to, he decided he had had enough. The bedroom door opened and Harry stood as he had done previously, only this time he had his belt wrapped around his knuckles with the buckle hanging down past his large gut. Mikey stood up, legs like jelly, and gritted his teeth. Harry walked towards him with sheer anger in his eyes and raised his arm up behind him. In the split second it took for Harry to swing the belt down, Mikey kicked him in the shin with everything he had but it wasn't enough to stop the momentum of the swing, and the belt hit Mikey on the top of his head sending him to the floor. He looked up clutching his head and saw Harry raise his arm once more.

"I'm going to teach you a real lesson this time" Harry had a rage in his eyes.

Mikey leaned forward and grabbed Harry's leg with both hands, opening his mouth as wide as he could he sank his teeth in and bit him. Harry let out a loud howl and dropped both hands to clutch his leg. Mikey got to his feet and with Harry crouching down they were now at face level. Mikey, who had been taught by Charlie to defend himself when he had been bullied in the playground, had also learned many manoeuvres that Charlie had been adamant were not for the playground. The type of actions that were only to be used under certain circumstances and it seemed to Mikey that now was one of those times. He raised his arm, and in a fast, powerful, stabbing motion he poked Harry in the eyes with his index and middle finger. Harry howled again and stood upright. He staggered around the room with his hands covering his face shouting that he couldn't see. Mikey looked at the clear doorway and made a run for it. As he attempted to sneak past Harry, he grabbed a hold of him. They struggled and both of them stumbled to the floor. Mikey tried to scramble away but Harry managed to grip him with one hand and began punching him with the other. Mikey looked up and saw a lamp that had been smashed in the struggle. He picked up a sharp piece of porcelain and as Harry could barely see, he lifted it above him and stabbed Harry in the back. He released Mikey and cried out in agony shouting for Linda. Mikey ran out of the room and barged past Linda who was making her way up the stairs. He ran out of the house and down the street in the direction of Anna's. He kept on running until he was out of breath couldn't run anymore. As he sat down by the side of the road waiting for his breathing to return to normal, the tears began to roll down his cheeks. He hadn't cried in a long time, not even after a hard beating from Harry. He sat for a while thinking about Anna and why she would move away without telling him. He felt lost and had nowhere to turn to. He stood up and wiped the tears from his face. He knew the police would be on their way to pick him up so he decided to save them the trouble and started walking back to his foster parent's house. He arrived just in time to see Harry being placed into the ambulance. A neighbour pointed Mikey out to the police who were busy questioning Linda. They came over and Mikey was escorted into the back of the patrol car.

Due to the severity of the assault on his foster father, Mikey was placed into a secure children's home. The secure home was generally used to accommodate young offenders aged twelve to fifteen and was run by the local authority social services department. It was a home to some of the most vulnerable young teenagers in the area and although it had a bad reputation, it didn't faze Mikey in the slightest, anything was better than having to face Harry and Linda again. Mikey was the youngest in the home by a few months and the most susceptible to being bullied. All the boys in the home had come from rough backgrounds where most had been abused to some extent. There was the usual power struggle amongst them that you would find in almost any school playground and the staff would turn a blind eye to most of it. Mikey tried to keep to himself but he knew it was only a matter of time before the other boys started to show their authority. Since he arrived he had watched them push some of the other boys around and take their allowance money from them. One of the boys had made the mistake of grassing and found himself with a severe beating. Mikey was on his own when two of the older boys confronted him. He was cornered in the toilet one day and the two bullies started on him without saying a word. Mikey fought back. The punches and kicks the boys threw at him were nothing to what he had received from Harry. Mikey walked out of the toilet first and left the two bullies in a mess on the floor. As far as Mikey was concerned, that was the end of the matter but no, this drew the attention of older, harder boys that now saw Mikey as a threat. The more Mikey was taunted and bullied, the more he fought back. Before long Mikey had a reputation as one who was not to be messed with. This brought its own trouble as there would always be someone who wanted to relieve Mikey of this reputation. Every new boy who came to the secure home brought with them a bigger swagger and a larger chip on their shoulder. The staff didn't help the situation as they constantly wound the boys up at every opportunity. These were grown men who took pleasure in bullying and beating up vulnerable young boys that they were supposed to be helping. When a fight broke out between two of the boys, this gave the staff the opportunity to use force. Mikey dealt with it in his usual way, by inflicting as much damage as possible. Each incident that Mikey was involved in was noted on his record and resulted in the authorities finding it more difficult to place him in a new foster home. Mikey didn't mind the secure home, he would have been happy to stay there until he was of an age to leave, until he was informed that if he was still a resident of the secure home when he reached the age of fifteen, he would be transferred to a Young Offenders Institution. This was a facility run by the prison service and accommodated fifteen to twenty-one year olds. The way the other boys talked, the secure home was like a holiday camp compared to the institution. This information had a major effect on Mikey as he started to avoid the staff as much as possible and managed to stay out of trouble for a long time. Due to his sudden change in behaviour Mikey's social worker had allocated him the next available foster home. This could not come quick enough as a new 'hard case' had been brought into the unit. His name was Andrew Nicol, known to the boys as Pickles. Mikey had heard his nick-name mentioned a few times since being in the unit from other boys that had confrontations with him. As soon as the boy walked through the door, Mikey knew there would be trouble. He was slightly shorter than Mikey but stockier and had piercing eyes that felt as though they looked through you. It was only his first day and he was making an impression by putting in his demands on some of the younger boys in the unit. Mikey left him to it, he knew it was only a matter of time before their paths crossed and he wasn't looking for it, he went about his business as he had always done. It was only Pickles third day in the unit and he had heard enough talk about Mikey, he wasn't about to wait around, it was time to make his presence felt. Mikey was lying on his bed when his door swung open.

"I hear you're the top man around here" Pickles said smugly.

Mikey tried to get to his feet but Pickles lunged forward with a fist and it caught Mikey on the side of the face, he felt the sting immediately. Another fist came at him but Mikey managed to get out of the way and throw one of his own. The two boys traded punches until they both fell back onto the bed. Mikey was on top and grabbed Pickles by the hair and smashed the back of his head on the bed post. Mikey stood up as Pickles rolled onto the floor clutching the back of his head with both hands. Mikey was about to walk out of the room when he felt a sharp pain in the back of his calf. He turned to see Pickles with a blade in his hand. He crouched down to clutch his leg and saw the blood soaking through his trousers. He swung the blade again but Mikey managed to get out of the way. Pickles got to his feet and charged at Mikey. Mikey grabbed the wrist holding the blade and as the two boys wrestled to the floor, Pickles dropped the blade. Other boys had heard the commotion and alerted the staff. On arrival, they witnessed Mikey, now the aggressor, on top of Pickles throwing punch after punch to his head.

Mikey was taken to hospital to have his leg stitched up and his social worker came to visit. Mikey received the news that he had been dreading. Due to the severity of this latest incident, the authorities had decided that he would not be placed in a new foster home and added with the fabricated reports from the staff, Mikey would also not be allowed back in the unit. Following his release from hospital, he would be transferred immediately to a Young Offenders Institution. Mikey pleaded his case that Pickles had come for him and that he also produced the blade, but this was all to no avail as his social worker backed the staff's report and concluded that Mikey was difficult and hard to control.

The Young Offenders Institution was set up after the previous organisation known as Borstal was officially closed in 1982. To boys like Mikey who unfortunately found themselves in the system, the Young Offenders Institution would still be known as Borstal.

Chapter 2

A new project was in the process of being set up, which had started the previous year to Mikey being sent to the Young Offenders Institution. It involved an active social worker named Brian Malliff. Brian had come up with the idea of the project several years before and had gradually worked to gain the interest and backing from the appropriate authorities. The project was titled 'The Program' and consisted of a home to cater for no more than ten selected candidates. Including Brian, there would be three full time staff. This was not a place where the worst offenders could go to avoid being detained in an institution. The Program would be set in a relaxed environment were the chosen candidates would be trusted to abide by the rules. Brian had grown up with the same background of abuse, violence and crime as with most of the kids that he worked with. It was during a spell in prison that he decided to put his life on the straight and narrow and began to study. After his release he worked as a volunteer to advise troubled teenagers that appeared to be going down the same path by making the wrong choices that he had. Brian was eventually awarded with a permanent position and over the years, he worked with some of the worst cases any social worker could come across. Through his help and advice, some of these teenagers had managed to turn their lives around, although this was not an overnight transition. Brian worked with them in all aspects of their life by helping them change their whole attitude and outlook towards other people and themselves.

Before the boys were selected for the program, Brian would study their files and backgrounds of boys that had a possibility of reforming. He would work with them to create an environment where they would be under no pressure from outside influences, but if they broke the rules they would not be given a second chance and would be sent straight back to the institution.

Over the years Brian had received awards and praise for his work and dedication in helping these vulnerable teenagers. When the decision came to award the funding for The Program, all the board members had agreed, all accept one. The only objection had come from Councillor Williamson. This was a vicious, ruthless man who ran the council with an iron fist. He had gone on record to say that he thought The Program was a waste of public money and that it was destined to fail. Putting all these violent teenagers in one place to roam free and cater for themselves was in no way going to change them into becoming decent law abiding citizens. Councillor Williamson had an ulterior motive to his objection. He had a history with Brian and did not like the fact that he had once been a criminal himself who was now considered a respected member of society. The funds that were set aside for The Program had been promised to Williamson only several months previously for one of his own useless promotional projects. After many meetings and long discussions, the board had decided to fund The Program for two years. The turning point for the Board was that if The Program was successful after the first two years, a local businessman would fund it for the next three. Williamson now had an axe to grind with the other board members as they voted in favour of Brian's project.

Accommodation for The Program was a purpose built unit on the outskirts of Dundee, far away from any scheme where the boys could be easily influenced. The building was set in a large area surrounded by fields and had two separate dorms for the boys which were set out in an army style barracks. A class room, a large lounge, three separate supervisors rooms, a kitchen with dining area, toilets, shower rooms and an office. A small mini bus was also privately funded for The Program. At the recommendation of Councillor Williamson, two full time wardens and one part time warden were employed for security reasons and paid for separately by Williamson's department. He insisted this was for Brian and the boys' safety, but everyone involved knew their priority was to report back to Williamson. The Councillor would never give The Program a chance and insisted on random visits and reports each week from the security wardens.

There were constant complaints by the boys about the two full time wardens, Frank and Bruce, who were bullying them when Brian was not around. As they were not officially employed by The Program, Brian had no authority over them and they had no say in how he ran it. Each complaint the boys made to Brian about the wardens, he had taken a note of the name, date, time and details in a note book and filed it away. The yearly review of The Program was coming up and Brian was intending on producing his notebook at the board meeting.

Brian's notebook containing all the details of Frank and Bruce's abuse was constantly kept under lock and key, he had still not found a member of the board that he trusted to disclose the information. He knew he had to tackle the problem soon as the boys on The Program were vulnerable, and if one of the warden's abuses went too far, these boys could easily kick off and retaliate. This would suit Councillor Williamson as the whole Program would be shut down. Brian knew the Councillor was behind the warden's actions but he did not have proof, and as all the other board members were afraid of him, he had no choice but to hold on. Every time Brian enquired about the wardens he was immediately shot down from none other than Councillor Williamson. He was not afraid of Williamson but without any other board member to back him, he would be putting The Program in jeopardy. After another disappointing board meeting, Brian headed out of the council chambers sharpish to catch the lift to the ground floor. In his rush he had not noticed that Rosie, one of Councillor Williamson's assistants was waiting close by. She entered the lift behind him and once the doors closed, she handed Brian a folded piece of paper.

"What's this?"

"It's a copy of a proposal that Barney put forward at the same time as your program."

"Who's Barney?"

"Councillor Williamson."

"No wonder he insists on people calling him Council-lor."

"It's actually short for Barnaby."

"Barnaby" Brian smiled.

"You mentioned the security guys on your program." Rosie continued

"Yeah" Brian said.

"Look I can't say too much at the moment but I know everything that's happening on your Program. Let's just say that I know it would be in Barney's best interest if The Program fails."

"Thanks for this" The lift chimed as it hit the ground floor and Brian took a step closer to the door but before he exited, he turned back,

"Excuse me, but is there any particular reason why you are getting involved?"

"Yes, but I can't tell you at the moment, all I can say is that you are not alone on The Program."

Brian smiled as he walked off, but was confused by his new found ally.

When Williamson walked out of the meeting he felt close to an anxiety attack. He hated Brian Malliff and thought the ex-criminal had no right to even be in his presence. The Program wasn't meant to last two months but it had been running for nearly a year with glowing reports, and now Brian Malliff was starting to ask questions about his wardens. He would have to step up the pressure. The Program had to fail and he would get rid of Brian Malliff, whatever it would took.

Brian was constantly being handed files of boys that had been detained or were about to be detained in the Young Offenders Institution. After looking over their past crimes and background checks, more than half were handed back without a second look. These were boys who were destined for a life of crime with or without his help and only time would tell if the institution would make or break them.

The next boy who was about to leave The Program was Graham Harvey. He had turned sixteen and was now officially allowed to leave. He had been in the Young Offenders Institution for over a year when Brian picked him for The Program. He had showed potential while in the institution and Brian had requested that he spend his remaining time on The Program. Due to Harvey's soon departure, Brian had his regular weekly meeting where he discussed the progress of all the boys and also to inform them of a new candidate that he had chosen for The Program.

Chapter 3

In the early Borstal days the wardens took it upon themselves to hand out severe physical punishments for petty rule breaking. When the Young Offenders Institutions was introduced, the governors placed the responsibility onto the older boys to hand out the beatings. The Young Offenders Institution was intended for vulnerable boys aged fifteen to twenty-one. Mikey, having only recently turned 14 was informed that he was only being placed there until the authorities could find another secure home to accommodate him. The nearest Institution was situated on the west coast of Scotland and had a bad reputation. Mikey was in the Institution for a little over a month and in that time he had been in front of the governor several times. At fourteen, Mikey was a stocky lad and along with his age and east coast accent, he was a target for bullies. Mikey had no fear and treated people the same way they treated him. If someone was civil, he would be civil back. If someone tried it on no matter how old or what size they were, he met them head on. The boys who did try it on were the usual run of the mill bad boys. In those first two weeks Mikey had proved to some of the older boys that he was more than capable of handling himself. By his third week, prior to being informed about The Program, he had gained some new acquaintances who had taken him under his wing.

Ronnie Martin was fifteen, a year older than Mikey but would easily pass as an eighteen year old. He was tall and stocky with large broad shoulders and came across as a simple boy which resulted in other boys trying to take a loan of him. Ronnie's parents were alcoholics and his childhood was spent taking beatings from his father on a regular basis. His mother was a wreck and she would also suffer at the hands of his father when Ronnie wasn't around. Ronnie would come home from school to see his mother with a black eye or a fat lip and this made him stop going to school. He wanted to be at home so that when his father felt the need to lash out, he would take the beating instead of his mother. The authorities were called every now and then and his father would get help.

Things would be okay for a while but it would gradually end up back in the same routine. As Ronnie got older the punches and kicks were not having the same effect, so the belt was introduced. At first, Ronnie felt like he was being whipped and his body would sting for days afterwards. Occasionally the buckle would break through Ronnie's skin and even though there would be blood seeping from his wounds, his father would still continue his onslaught. All through these years of abuse Ronnie hid the bruises and cuts. If someone happened to notice them he would make excuses and dream up bizarre stories to explain them. In his mind, if the authorities had found out the truth, he would have been taken into care leaving his mother to receive the beatings. Through his years of drunkenness, Ronnie's father had failed to notice that he was growing at a fast pace and by the time Ronnie reached fifteen, he was six foot tall. At school, when Ronnie did bother to turn up, he was nicknamed the gentle giant. The only time he got into trouble at school was for minor things like not doing his homework. He had a few friends but never anyone close enough that he could talk to. Ronnie did find himself a girlfriend, her name was Lesley-Ann Donnelly. She was a short red haired girl who lived close by and Ronnie began to open up to her about the true extent of his home life. She was shocked when he revealed the extent of the marks on his body but he made her swear not to tell a soul. She did tell her parents who immediately phoned the authorities, although his was not with the intention of helping Ronnie. Lesley-Ann's father's sole purpose was in the hope that Ronnie would be taken into care and thus, stopping their daughter's relationship with him. Social services once again intervened but as always Ronnie denied the marks were from abuse. After things had settled, his father started on him once again, and for what would be the last time.

Lesley-Ann was instructed not to see Ronnie anymore by her father but they would secretly meet up. One day, while they skipped school, she knew something was bothering Ronnie, he was quieter than usual but he would not tell her what was on his mind. During the afternoon they spent together Ronnie became more withdrawn as it came nearer time for them to return home. She knew it was something bad but she never asked. If Ronnie wanted to tell her he would do it in his own time. He walked into his house and was greeted with his father's drunken rage where he continually cursed and blamed Lesley-Ann for all the trouble she had brought to the family. Ronnie crouched into his usual corner with his father standing over him striking him again and again with a wooden table leg, all the while shouting obscenities directed at Lesley-Ann. Ronnie snapped. He stood up and faced his father. As he swung his arm to strike him once more, Ronnie pushed him, he stumbled back against the wall and Ronnie quickly grabbed the table leg and began hitting his father repeatedly. Ronnie's mother came through screaming and tried to stop him. He pushed her away in disgust and continued hitting his limp father all over his body. Due to his mother's screams a neighbour came running through and pulled Ronnie away. He dropped the table leg and sat in a corner of the room until the police arrived.

After Ronnie's onslaught, his father was in intensive care for two weeks. He was now in a wheelchair and required twenty four hour care for the rest of his life. Ronnie was not allowed to return home and was placed into temporary foster care. He was arrested and charged with attempted murder. At Ronnie's trial, his mother did not speak up for him and decided to stand by his father. She continued with the lie that Ronnie's attack on his father was unprovoked and Ronnie was found guilty. Prior to being sent to a Young Offenders Institution, Ronnie was appointed a new social worker. He looked at Ronnie's case and the background of abuse that had never been fully investigated. He requested that Ronnie be allowed to take part in a new rehabilitation program that was being set up. That social worker was Brian Malliff.

Brian had travelled through to the Institution in the minibus and had taken Ronnie with him. It was a couple of hours drive and having Ronnie with him would maybe help Mikey feel more at ease on the journey back to Dundee. Mikey was already in the reception area when Brian arrived. The governor had already informed Mikey about The Program and the reasons why he was chosen. After all the trouble Mikey had been in since he arrived, the governor actually smiled at him, shook his hand and wished Mikey good luck, this was also accompanied with some advice of never returning. Mikey wondered if he gave the same speech to every person who left. Brian smiled and introduced himself, while Mikey, unsure of where or what he was moving onto, did not smile but lifted his head in acknowledgement. He picked up his small holdall containing all his worldly possession and walked with Brian back out to the minibus, where an anxious Ronnie was waiting to introduce himself. Brian knew it was a good idea to bring him along with him as the two talked for most of the journey home.

Chapter 4

Brian had been out of the camp for most of the day, and as usual, he was worried about leaving his boys under the watch of the security wardens. He had found a pattern to the bullying. It was only when Frank and Bruce were on a shift together that something happened. Today Scott was on. Scott was good with the boys, he was ex-army and wasn't one for standing around. His job was to supervise, but most of the time he got involved with whatever was going on and Brian thought he could do with a few more staff like him. As he drove into the grounds of the camp, the rest of the boys were outside kicking a ball around, but it appeared that two of them were more interested in kicking each other.

"Will I take Mikey over to meet the rest of the boys Brian?" Ronnie said as he climbed out of the minibus.

"No, Ronnie you go and join them. I'm going to show Mikey around the place and explain the rules of The Program."

"Okay, I'll see you in a while Mikey."

As Ronnie walked over, two of the other boys were close to a punch up, Robbo and Alonso. Matty, one of the other boys stepped in between them to calm them down. Brian didn't say anything as he was pre-occupied with his new arrival, although he would have words with them later as their niggling at each other was becoming more than a daily occurrence.

"More trouble coming our way Ronnie?" Paul asked as he stood holding the ball while he waited for the game to start again.

"Hope it's not another Paki" Robbo said as he tried to reach over and slap Alonso.

"I'm Chilean you racist prick."

"Oh I'm not a Paki, I'm Chilean" Robbo said putting on a squeaky voice.

"Give it a break Robbo. If Brian catches you saying that you'll be in big trouble man." Ronnie stepped in to help split them up. He grabbed hold of Robbo and dragged him away.

"Get your hands off me you fucking mug."

Ronnie let him go but stood in front of him and Robbo put on his hard man stance with his arms out wide to square up to him. Ronnie laughed at him and walked away.

"Yeah you had better walk away before I…"

Ronnie turned back around and looked as though he was about to run at Robbo, he took a quick couple of steps and Robbo ran off. Ronnie turned back around to the other boys and they all laughed. He knew he wouldn't hit Robbo and so did the other boys, only Robbo didn't know this.

Robbo, whose real name was John Robertson, was one of the first boys to be considered for The Program, but this was not due to him committing any serious crimes or that the authorities were about to lock him up, it was at his father's request. Robbo's father was a very rich man and had a considerable amount of influence with the councillors on the board. When he heard about The Program, it was at a time when he was having extreme difficulty with his son. He had inside knowledge by one of the other councillors that the funding for The Program was about to be rejected by Williamson, so Robbo's father put forward a proposal that if The Program was successful after its initial two year trial, he would fund it for a further three. The only condition was that a placement was reserved for his son as he was becoming something of an embarrassment. Robbo's father wanted Brian to give his son some direction in his life before he ended up in prison. Due to Robbo's father's proposal, the board had no option but to vote in favour of Brian's Program.

Since Robbo was a young age, he had always been the type of boy who sized people up and tried to prove he was the hardest and best fighter. He walked with the biggest swagger and talked and acted like a would-be hard man. He was constantly being thrown out of school or picked up by the police and most of the incidents related to assault. After latching onto a group of boys who went to watch football games, his father thought this was a good thing as he started taking an interest in his appearance by wearing the latest designer clothes. It wasn't until he received a phone call that his son had been picked up and charged with racism and soccer violence that he realised his son was becoming a football casual.

Alonso Uribe's parents came to Britain from Chile in South America. They had travelled with their two young sons Cristian and Pedro. Alonso was born several years later in Scotland. During Cristian and

Pedro's time growing up in Dundee, they had endured the standard name calling and abuse just like many other ethnic families. They handled it well by choosing to ignore most of it, but not Alonso. He handled it in his own way, through violence. His parents were constantly being called up to his school due to him fighting with other pupils or arguing with teachers who he claimed were picking on him. He had switched schools so many times his parents were close to sending him over to family in Chile to live. Alonso was a very intelligent boy and because of this his parents gave him chance after chance to stop resorting to violence. Alonso was given counselling to help him deal with his problems and this worked for a short time until another disagreement with his maths teacher Mr. Kelly had got out of hand. He was sent out of the class and the teacher followed. He closed the door behind him and slapped Alonso hard across the back of the head. Alonso turned around and stood rooted to the spot in shock.

"Come on then. Where's your big mouth now?" The teacher said with his wide scary eyes. Alonso couldn't speak, his mouth had gone dry and his chest felt tight. Mr. Kelly lifted his hand again and this time slapped Alonso across the face. This sent him to the floor. Alonso cowered away in fear. Mr Kelly stormed over and grabbed Alonso by the neck lifting him up and pinning him against the wall. With his face only inches away from him, Alonso could smell his rotting breath when he said; "You're not so mouthy now are you? You little Paki bastard"

The grip around Alonso's neck became tighter and he began to choke. Alonso thought he was about to pass out when he heard the tip tap of a woman's heals coming along the corridor. It was Miss Ferrie, Alonso's guidance teacher. He felt relieved that now he had a witness to him being assaulted. Mr Kelly released his grip slightly but kept him pinned to the wall.

"What's going on?" Miss Ferrie asked.

"This little Paki has just lashed out at me."

"What? I never did anything. You sent me out of the class and hit me."

"Now Alonso, I don't think Mr. Kelly would hit you. Accusations like that could get you into a lot of trouble."

"But you've just heard him call me a Paki."

"I don't think so."

Alonso couldn't believe what he was hearing. He had been bullied and picked on for many years and the very people who were supposed to be helping him had now turned against him.

"But Miss you just heard him."

Mr. Kelly looked at Alonso with a smug grin and the fear in Alonso turned to anger. Alonso snapped. He grabbed one of Mr. Kelly's fingers and pulled it back as hard as he could. Mr Kelly let out a squeal and the grip was released from around his neck. Alonso didn't let go, Mr. Kelly was soon on his knees begging him to let go. Alonso snapped it back with a force and heard the bone crack.

"I'm going to kill you, you dirty little Paki" He shouted as he crumbled to the floor clutching his hand.

Alonso turned and ran.

"I'm Chilean you stupid fuck."

He ran out of the school and all the way home. Alonso's father was outraged and had his coat on ready to march back up to the school with him. As they left the house a police car pulled up and Alonso was charged with assault. He was thrown out of school once again and told to attend a panel hearing. The panel is a place where volunteers from the community, social workers, parents and teachers sit around a table and discuss what would be the best course of action for youngsters who have found themselves in trouble. On deciding Alonso's future, other teachers who were not present at the time of the assault, had now come forward to tell a fictional report of what happened. Mr. Kelly's injuries were somewhat exaggerated to the extent that he claimed he could not use his hand again properly. Alonso was made out to be a thug that was fast becoming out of control. Due to Alonso's record, the panel had believed the teachers version of events. He had been transferred from so many schools that his parents were now starting to doubt him. The panel decided that a short spell in a Young Offenders Institution would maybe help control his violent temper.

Brian had read Alonso's file a number of times before stepping in. He did a background check on Mr. Kelly, something the children's panel had never bothered to do. He found that he had a small file of complaints against him from previous students, each one accusing him of assaulting them. He was confused as to why a boy who worked hard, had top grades in every class would suddenly attack a teacher for no reason, something didn't add up. He tried to speak to Alonso's parents and get them to appeal the decision but they had washed their hands of him and believed that a spell in a Young Offenders Institution would maybe sort out his anger issues. Although Brian couldn't change the panel's decision, he fought Alonso's case hard and his request was granted to transfer Alonso on to The Program.

Chapter 5

Paul Connelly, was going to be Brian's biggest challenge. Paul was not a fighter, he didn't have a hard upbringing, he hadn't committed any serious crime, but he had constantly been in trouble since he was a very young age. His minor crimes were consistent enough to be put in front of the children's panel, many times. Every time he appeared, he had been given a warning and informed that this was his last chance. It was one last chance too many as the panel's patience had worn out and they decided that it would be best if he spent some time in a Young Offenders Institution. Paul, due to his size was being bullied on a daily basis by the other boys at the Institution, until Ronnie arrived. Ronnie took to Paul straight away and became his unofficial bodyguard. When Brian had turned up at the Institution to interview Ronnie for The Program, Ronnie had requested that Brian take look at Paul's file. Ronnie had feared that Paul would not survive if he left.

On reading Paul's file, Brian noticed that each report on him had stated that he was easily led. He had come from a good family that had gone to great lengths to help him, but Paul continued to find himself in trouble. When Brian met Paul he found him to be a funny, likeable boy. The first thing he noticed was his innocent smile which he found unusual for someone who was constantly in trouble. Most of the boys that Brian came across with a record like Paul's, would have the typical swagger and an attitude that Brian could relate to, but not Paul. He was the type of boy where everything in life was about having fun, only Paul's version of fun would be considered mischief. He could understand now why he was given chance after chance from the children's panel. In each case Paul pleaded that he was just in the wrong place at the wrong time and now, after meeting him he could see why he would be believed. Paul had a knack of latching onto the wrong crowd, a crowd that were stealing and breaking into places as they had nothing and had come from families that had nothing. But Paul was different. His family provided him with everything he ever needed. One of the reports that made Brian request Paul for the program was by a social worker, who, many years ago, had stated that Paul was not easily led but that he was the leader. He was an intelligent boy who had specifically picked out friends that made him appear to be the one led astray. Whatever the situation was, he knew Paul would be a difficult case to crack. He was either a naïve boy who needed some direction or a very intelligent boy with a total disregard for any figure of authority.

    Brian was handed another large stack of files from his assistant. He sat down at his desk and worked his way through them. Most had been put in a pile to be returned and occasionally there would be one that needed further reading. When he came across Mathew Brown's file, he glanced at the boy's record and was ready to put it aside until he read more. Mathew was the stereotypical hard case. He came from a family of petty criminals. His father and older brothers had, or were still doing time in jail and Mathew would soon be following them. Most boys with files like Mathew's wouldn't be given a second look. He would put the files aside as he knew that most of them would think the program was just an easy way out from being detained in the Institution. With these types of boys, Brian could spend two years on the program with them and they would still leave to go and continue a life of crime. Brian had been around long enough to know if a person had an attitude that was capable of being changed. If the program was to be successful, Brian needed a boy who looked to be beyond help and Mathew's whole life of crime had been all mapped out since the day he was born. As he picked up the file he knew of Mathew's family from his own previous life of crime. The more he read the more he came to relate to the boy. Mathew had decent grades when he attended school and although he was always in trouble outside of school, his reports from teachers were good enough to persuade Brian that he wanted Mathew on The Program. If he could get through to someone like Mathew, maybe his influence could rub off on some of the other boys. Mathew had seen first-hand what a life of crime actually involved, as when he was a young boy, he was taken by his mother to visit his father in many different prisons around the country. As he grew older he was making the same trips to visit his older brothers. If Brian managed to turn someone like Mathew's life around, The Program would be a hailed as a success.

Chapter 6

During dinner the night Mikey arrived, Brian introduced each of the other boys as they sat around the table, and in turn, they nodded their head in Mikey's direction. The dinner was served by Paul and Alonso. They all took turns at cooking their main meal each night. It was simple meals but it gave the boys some sort of responsibility while learning to do things for themselves. The boys were paired off alternatively so that they worked with someone different each time. The only two who had not worked together were Alonso and Robbo. Brian knew they needed more time to work on Robbo's racist attitude before pairing them together.

Later that night Brian had organised a discussion group. Each week they all sat down together and talked about anything that was bothering them on The Program and put forward anything they would like to see happen. This was intended to be a serious discussion but most of the time it ended in Brian laughing with the boys as they moaned about each other's annoying habits.

"I would like to make a complaint about Ronnie" Paul said.

"What! What have I done now?"

"Hold it Ronnie, let him speak. That's what the discussion group is for" Brian said.

"I would like to request that Ronnie be made to sleep in the other dorm on his own."

"Yeah, me too, I mean we all have to fart but my bunk is straight across from Ronnie's and he waft's the covers so that the smell comes directly to me" Robbo said.

"Guys, it's only when you feed me soup for lunch, if you put too much vegetables in there, they make me fart" Ronnie pleaded.

"Yeah but you don't have to waft it in my face."

"Well I don't want it to linger about in my bed, do I?"

Brian laughed but his smile dropped when he looked at Mikey who had no expression.

"What do you think Mikey, how do you suppose we resolve this?" Brian said to include Mikey in the discussion.

Mikey looked around the room at everyone as they stared at him.

"Stop feeding the big dopey bastard" He said as he smiled at Ronnie.

They all laughed as Ronnie grabbed Mikey in a head lock and they playfully wrestled around the room. Brian sat back and smiled, thus confirming to himself that picking Mikey was a good choice for The Program.

Over the next few days Mikey settled in well on The Program, although the busy work schedule and educational side of the program was not what he was expecting. Mikey noticed that most of the boys went out of their way to make him feel welcome, all except Matty, who had now taken over Harvey's roll of team leader. This meant that he was now responsible for giving out the work details for the week and making sure the rest of the boys were doing their chores properly. On Mikey's first night of making dinner for everyone he was paired off with Paul. As Paul got on with the task, Mikey stood around reluctant to help.

"I'm not here to cook for everyone."

"Hey, we are all here to muck in and help each other. Everyone has to take a turn."

"I have never cooked anything in my life."

"Its easy mate, I'll do most of it and I'll show you things as we go. Here, you can chop these tomatoes, you know how to chop tomatoes don't you?"

"What's this place all about? How is learning to cook going to stop anybody from getting into trouble?"

"Hey Mikey we are all here for the same reasons you are. What was it? A broken home, in with the wrong crowd, petty crime, stealing, drugs, fighting, stabbing..."

Mikey looked up when Paul mentioned stabbing.

"Stabbing" Paul repeated before he raised his eye-brows at Mikey and looked at the knife he was holding.

"Well I never actually..." Mikey attempted to plead his case when Paul reached over and took the kitchen knife from him.

"I'll just get you to grate some cheese okay?" Paul said seriously.

They both looked at each other and started laughing as Mikey realised Paul was only winding him up.

Early the next day, the English tutor arrived, so the boys gathered in the classroom. As the boys had different levels of education, they were all left to carry on with their own work while the tutor attended to their individual needs. Mikey sat at the back and the teacher introduced herself. She had never met Mikey and asked him to complete a set of tasks to find out what level he was at. Mikey completed the tests in half the time allocated and looked on as Robbo read to the rest of the boys. He struggled with some of the more difficult words but was helped along by the teacher.

"Well done John, that's coming along. Michael you appear to have finished, would you like to start where John finished off."

"Not really" Mikey said.

"Excuse me Michael but you were requested on this Program so that we could try to educate you and teach you how to show some respect. This is for your benefit to show the authorities that you are better than what they perceive you to be. We believe and trust that you are not the type of person whose future lies in prison. Now take the book and start where John left off or I will inform Brian that you would like to spend the rest of your time in the Institution."

Mikey stood up and walked to the front of the class. He picked up the book from the table and began to read faultlessly. He read two paragraphs and put the book down.

"Do you want me to continue?"

"No I think you have proved your point" The tutor smiled.

After looking at the results of Mikey's tests and hearing his reading skills, the tutor started him on the same level of course work as Matty, who was until now, considered the more intelligent of the group.

A few weeks had passed and Mikey was gradually settling into life on The Program. He began to place his trust in Brian and saw him more as a friend than a figure of authority. Mikey only had one problem with The Program, it was the same problem that the other boys had, and that was with the two security staff, Frank and Bruce. One night when Brian was called away to an important meeting, Frank and Bruce were left in charge. The boys had finished their chores that Brian had set them to do while he was away and they were gathered in the lounge watching TV. Mikey went into the kitchen to make himself a sandwich, when Frank appeared. He stood in the doorway and waited until Mikey had finished then casually walked over, picked up his plate and tilted it until the sandwich fell on the floor.

"Oops" Frank said.

Mikey looked at him confused.

"Pick it up then" Frank stared at him with menacing eyes.

Mikey had seen that stare many times in the past. It usually meant trouble. Mikey stood rooted to the spot unsure of Frank's intentions. He squared up to him.

"Come on then. If you're going to do something, do it. Let's see how hard you think you are."

Ronnie walked into the kitchen.

"What's going on?"

Mikey and Frank's faces were only inches from each other.

Frank took a step back. "Clean it up" He smirked at Mikey and walked out of the kitchen.

Ronnie saw the rage in Mikey's eyes and looked down at his clenched fists.

"Don't let him get to you Mikey, that's what he wants."

Ronnie picked up the sandwich and put it in the bin.

"What the hell was that all about?"

"We don't know. They try it on with all of us, only when Brian is not around."

"Why don't you tell Brian?"

"We have, each one of us has mentioned it to him but because it happens when we are on our own, it is our word against theirs. Brian knows what's going on and says he knows why they are doing it but he needs proof. He told us he was trying his best to get rid of them but his hands are tied at the moment"

Chapter 7

After another pointless meeting with the board, Brian was in a rush to get out of the building and back to the camp. He knew the boys had been left under the supervision of Frank and Bruce, and that any one of them could kick off at any time. He had told the boys in secret not to be left alone in their company. He hadn't mentioned it to Mikey though as he thought it best to let him settle in before letting him know what was going on. Brian was about to enter the lift when Rosie, his newly acquired friend caught up with him. They did not speak until they entered the lift and the door closed.

"How is your evidence going?"

"Not so good, my boys are being bullied by my security staff that I have no say over and I can't even make a formal complaint. As soon as I bring them up at the meetings I am cut off by Williamson and none of the rest of the board will speak up to help me out. Does he not realise I am trying to help these boys"

"Look just hold tight and tell your boys to stay calm. I am working on it. If I am caught going behind Barney's back I will be out of a job."

The lift stopped and so did the conversation. They stood apart when someone entered. The lift reached the ground floor and before Brian exited, Rosie slipped a piece of paper into his pocket. On the way to the car park Brian put his hand into his pocket for his car keys and found the piece of paper.

Graham Harvey received £1000 in his bank account from council funds and has been offered a permanent job in Councillor Williamson's department.

Brian stood outside the minibus and read the note over again before it sunk in. Williamson was paying Harvey to keep his mouth shut. Two thousand is not a lot of money but to a sixteen year old it was a fortune. Brian knew he had to get back to the camp as soon as possible but he made a quick detour to pay a visit to Harvey.

Prior to Harvey leaving the program, Brian had looked at his situation and was informed that he could not return home as his parents did not want him there. Upon leaving The Program, Brian set him up in a small flat and found him a job. As he was the first to leave The Program it was imperative that Harvey stayed on the straight and narrow.

Brian arrived at the flat and knocked on the door.

"Hi Brian, how is it going?"

"Graham, can I have a word?"

"Sure, come in. Sounds serious"

Brian walked into the flat and straight away he clocked the new TV and stereo.

"Not working today?"

"No, I eh, handed in my notice. I have a new job, I start next week. I thought you would have known about it."

"Why would I know about it?"

"Well it's with the council. Some really big guy said he wanted to try and help out with The Program and find us decent jobs."

"I see you have been treating yourself" Brian said as he nodded in the direction of the TV and stereo.

"Yeah, I eh, got offered an advance if I took the job."

Through Brian's years of experience he was able to tell when someone was lying by their tone of voice, their actions or even just by the look in their eyes. He knew straight away that Harvey was lying but he didn't push it. He had so many questions he wanted to ask Harvey but he knew most of the answers would be lies. Who approached him about the job? Who offered him the money? What has he promised to say or not to say?

"Graham I need to know something."

"Sure, what's up?"

"The notes I took during our one to one sessions, you know, the ones I have locked away."

"Uh huh, what about them"

"You signed a complaints statement against Frank and Bruce do you remember?"

"Eh, Yeah, of course, but it was nothing really. I mean, my head was really mixed up during those sessions."

Brian suddenly realised that he could not count on Harvey as a witness and felt angry and betrayed. More important to him was just how much he had said about the complaints book. Williamson had obviously covered himself with the bribe by calling it an advance. He now had other things to worry about. Harvey's new job, how long will he last before he is set up for stealing or some other petty crime? Brian got up to leave. He knew he had to act soon.

"Oh eh, Graham, you wouldn't happen to have mentioned those notes to anyone else would you?"

"No, why would I?"

Brian looked Harvey straight in the eye. It was an-other lie.

It was still sunny when Brian arrived back at the camp even though it was late, but the boys were all inside. He walked straight to his office and took out his key to unlock it. Ronnie walked past and gave him a look.

"Mikey" Brian asked.

Ronnie nodded.

Brian walked through to the lounge.

"Mikey, can I talk to you for a minute?"

"Yeah sure"

Mikey followed Brian through to his office.

"Take a seat."

"What's this about?"

"Is there anything you want to tell me?"

Mikey shrugged. "I don't think so. Why, what's up?"

"Did anything happen today that I should know about?"

Mikey looked around the office, at the walls, the ceiling and back to the walls before eventually locking eyes with Brian.

"Are you referring to the incident in the kitchen earlier, where one of your security wardens was close to getting his face smashed in. If you are referring to that then yeah, I think maybe you should know about it."

Brian sat back in his chair.

"I'm really sorry Mikey. I should have warned you about what was going on. It's been happening to all the boys here. They are employed by a separate department from The Program. I know who is behind it, but I can't prove it yet. They want The Program to fail."

"Is there anything we could do?"

"Yes. Nothing, I really need you guys to try to control yourselves and not kick off if they start."

"I have a lot of respect for you Brian and I can see what you are trying to do for us with The Program and all, but I'm sorry, I can't promise that. All I can say is that I will try my best."

"That's all I ask."

During the night Ronnie got up to use the bath-room and as he stood relieving himself, Bruce entered. He walked over to Ronnie and pushed him from behind. This resulted in Ronnie dribbling on the floor.

"Ronald, look what you have gone and done, you big retard" Bruce said with a smug grin.

Ronnie looked at him but did nothing. Bruce pushed him again and Ronnie stumbled back and slipped in his own urine before falling on the floor. Bruce kicked him in the stomach and slapped him in the head.

"Look at the mess you've made. Clean it up."

Bruce grabbed his hair and pushed his face to the floor.

"Come on then retard."

Ronnie lay on the wet floor gritting his teeth. He was ready to explode. There was only so much he could take. The handle on the door made a noise and Bruce stood up and took a step back. Mikey entered.

"What's going on? Are you okay Ronnie?"

"He's fine, he's had a bit of an accident. Clean yourself up and get back to bed." Bruce said as walked out of the bathroom.

Ronnie watched as Mikey squared up to Bruce on his way out. Bruce smirked and walked past him. Mikey picked up a towel, threw it on the floor and offered his hand to help Ronnie up.

"Thanks mate."

"No problem, I owed you one."

They both cleaned up and headed back to their beds. In the morning Frank left and was replaced by Scott who was welcomed with big smiles from all the boys.

On finishing his shift at the camp Frank was ordered to attend a meeting with his boss at the council offices. He walked into the reception and was met by the long stern faces of Williamson's unhappy workforce. The receptionist announced on the phone that he had arrived and he was ushered through straight away.

"What the hell is going on at that camp? I have been expecting to hear news that one of those little shits have lashed out and attacked one of you. But all I ever hear is glowing reports of how they are passing exams and behaving like choir boys. I paid you and your sidekick to do a job, now why haven't you done it."

"We've tried, they won't react. Brian must have warned them."

"Well I guess we will have to go to plan B."

"What's plan B?"

"Brian Malliff"

"What, we start on him?"

"No, those boys will start on him, and you and Bruce will witness it. If you know what I mean"

"You mean we do some damage and blame it on them."

"Now you're getting it."

"But that means we would have to do a proper job so that he won't be capable of defending them."

"If that's what it takes."

"I think you need to make it clear what you're asking us to do here."

Williamson threw a fat envelope on his desk. "I think this is enough to know what I'm asking."

Frank leaned over and picked it up. He looked inside and smiled. "I think this makes it pretty clear what you're asking."

"Good. Oh, and just so that you know, he has a notebook filled with complaints about you and Bruce. Each and every time you did anything to those boys has been recorded, dated and signed by each boy."

"What? The sneaky bastard"

"I suggest you get your hands on that before you do anything."

"How do you know all this?"

"From our newly acquired employee"

"Harvey" Frank smirked.

They both smiled at each other and Frank walked out of the office holding the envelope tightly.

Chapter 8

Over the next week, Brian had been putting his evidence together and was about to go above Williamson's head with his complaints. On the morning of the shift change over, Scott was replaced by Bruce. Brian noticed that Scott was acting very strange. He tried to get him on his own to talk but as Bruce arrived, Scott left without saying a word. There was a trip planned into town that day as Brian promised Mikey he would get him kitted out with some new clothes. Brian had done this for some of the other boys who had arrived at the camp with little more than the clothes on their back. With Frank and Bruce on a shift together, Brian decided to take all the boys with him in the minibus.

The boys only ever left the camp for specific reasons and it was usually to help with shopping or visits with their families. For them to be all together on a trip into town was a big deal for them. There was the usual teasing and wind-ups between the boys during the journey but it was all in good fun. Brian could see that the boys were happy and excited to be away from the camp for the day. After a quick shopping spree where Mikey was constantly teased for his chosen attire, Brian decided to treat them to lunch. With large plates of junk food all around, Brian sat back in his chair and watched as the boys laughed and joked among themselves. Just over six months ago some of these boys were destined for a term in an Institution, a breeding ground for future hard core criminals. He knew he had chosen the correct boys for The Program and even though Robbo's racist attitude was still a problem, Brian knew that it could be dealt with over time. Brian treated them to another round of drinks before they walked back through the town towards the mini bus. The boys were quiet on the journey home and Brian knew it was because they were about to be faced with Frank and Bruce. With the effort that these boys had shown in reforming, he knew the time had come to deal with this head on.

They arrived back at the camp and Brian headed straight to his office. As soon as he sat down at his desk he knew something was not right. He noticed that some of his things had been moved around and the drawers had been upturned. The locks on his filling cabinet had been forced open and when he searched for his complaints book. It was gone. He was ready to storm out and confront Frank and Bruce but he stood and took several deep breaths until he calmed down. The last thing he wanted was for his boys to see him become angry and aggressive after everything he had tried to teach them. He made a decision to wait until the morning and confront the board with what evidence he had and ask for an investigation. Brian made a phone call and caught the council offices before closing. He requested an emergency meeting with the board for the next morning and the message was passed on to Williamson.

"Is everything okay Brian?" Ronnie asked as he appeared from his office.

"Yeah of course, why"

"You look a little stressed."

"No, I'm fine. I just have a few things on my mind." Brian looked over at the two wardens as they whispered between themselves.

"Oh right, I see what you mean."

During the evening Frank received an anonymous phone call where he was informed about the emergency meeting. He was told that whatever it took, the meeting must not take place.

Only a few hours after going to bed, Mikey woke with a sudden urge to use the toilet. He stumbled through the dark until he reached the hallway. As he walked through to the bathroom he overheard some raised voices from Brian's office. On the way back he creeped lightly towards the office door and heard some dull noises and a low whimpering.

"Where is it?" Bruce said in an angry tone.

There was another dull smacking sound and then a whimper. Mikey opened the door handle slowly and peaked around. Frank and Bruce had their backs to the door and through the gap Mikey could see Brian tied to his chair with a rag shoved in his mouth. His face was swollen and blood was dripping down from his head. Mikey was frozen to the spot and looked on in shock. Bruce raised a steel bar and held it in front of Brian's face.

"You have one last chance. Where is the notebook?"

Brian saw Mikey through the gap and they locked eyes with each other. Bruce took a large swing with the bar and it crunched into the side of Brian's head, it snapped to the side and his blood splattered against the wall. Mikey opened the door further and Frank turned to see him standing with his eyes wide and his mouth open. Frank reached over and grabbed Mikey by his t-shirt. Mikey stepped back and pulled the door closed on his arm. He kept a tight grip on his t-shirt but Mikey leaned forward and sunk his teeth into the back of Frank's hand which made him release his grip. Mikey ran across the hall and back into the boys' dorm. He put on the light and ran towards his bunk. As he started to push it towards the door, the rest of the boys woke up.

"Come on, help me" He shouted.

Ronnie was the first to get up and help him without even questioning why. The metal bunk was slammed tight against the door and Mikey hurried to the next one.

"What's going on?" Matty demanded.

"Frank and Bruce, they have Brian, he's covered in blood. Come on help me."

Frank tried to open the door and the first bunk was pushed slightly forward.

"Open the door" Frank shouted.

With the help of Bruce they gave the door a large shove and it opened far enough for Frank to slide his head through.

"Move the bed or I will kill the lot of you."

Robbo took a run from the other side of the room and Frank slid his head back just in time as the bed forced the door closed again. Ronnie, Mikey and Paul managed to pick up another bunk and lift it on top of the first one. The rest of the boys pushed all the beds towards the door, barricading them inside.

"What do we do now?" Alonso asked.

"Get something on your feet we will have to make a run for it" Mikey said.

"Wait a minute, I'm going nowhere I haven't done anything wrong" Matty said.

"Well you can stay here and tell them that, but I'm getting the hell out of here."

"How are you planning to do that?"

Mikey looked at the windows which were high up and only two foot square.

"You have got to be kidding."

As the boys quickly put on their jeans and trainers Frank and Bruce were taking it in turns to barge the door and the beds were moving slightly each time.

As soon as the boys were ready, Mikey began piling up the boys lockers near the window. Robbo noticed the door being opened further and Frank's arm was through the gap. He grabbed Ronnie and they both ran forward and pushed the beds back squashing Franks arm in the process. He let out a loud yelp before he managed to slide it back through. The boys took it in turns to help each other climb out of the window. Frank and Bruce started charging the door at the same time and Robbo was the last one trying to hold the beds in place. His heels were sliding backwards with each push.

"Come on you guys, hurry up. I can't hold it much longer."

The door opened enough for Frank to fit through and Robbo made a run for it. He climbed up the lockers against the wall and reached for the window. As he pulled himself up onto the ledge Frank grabbed his leg.

"Guys he's got my leg, help."

"Come on Ronnie" Alonso shouted as he ran back to the window.

Ronnie stood with his back against the wall and his hands clenched together. Alonso put his foot onto Ronnie's grasp and lifted himself up to the window. He grabbed Robbo's hands and pulled as hard as he could. Frank had a tight hold of Robbo's leg but as he was balancing on the lockers he had no support. Robbo used his other leg and continued kicking back. One of the kicks eventually landed on Frank's chest which pushed him off balance. He let go of Robbo to try and control his fall. Robbo stumbled out of the window and they all landed in a pile on the ground. As soon as they were on their feet they ran with the other boys as fast they could through the dark fields away from the camp. Bruce called the police and they were immediately alerted to be on the lookout for six teenage boys. Before the ambulance arrived, Frank wiped down any fingerprints on the steel bar and anything else that they could have touched while they were in Brian's office. Bruce put his head down to Brian's face.

"He's still breathing."

"Well?"

"Well what?"

"What are you waiting on?"

Bruce hesitated and then looked up at Frank.

"Out of the way" Franks said.

He moved down towards Brian and put his hand over his mouth and nose. Bruce stood up and watched as Brian's body jerked slightly several times before Frank got up and walked to the bathroom to wash the blood off his hands. Bruce followed him as they discussed their version of events so that their stories coincided. A police car pulled up and the ambulance arrived minutes later. They went straight to work untying him from the chair and once he was laid on the floor they gave him shock treatment to try and revive him. Frank and Bruce looked on from the hall outside as Brian was pronounced dead at the scene.

Detective Chief Inspector Smith was woken with the news that Brian Malliff had been attacked and killed by the boys in his care. He got out of bed and instead of his usual ritual of two mugs of strong coffee to help him face his daily events. He quickly got dressed and rushed out the door. He had known Brian for many years after he had contacted him for advice on various social work projects. He also had the opportunity to work alongside him and witnessed first-hand the respect some of the most vulnerable teenagers had for him. He found the news of his murder quite disturbing. As soon as he arrived on the scene he was introduced to Frank and Bruce and immediately took a dislike to them. He, like Brian, had been around long enough to know when someone was lying.

When Smith arrived back at the station he listened to the fictional statements of Frank and Bruce when they were interviewed.

"So you woke during the night to hear a noise coming from Brian's office. When you opened the door he was tied to a chair and one of the boys, McDonnell was it?"

"Yeah, Mikey McDonnell" Frank confirmed.

"He hit him over the head with a steel bar. That's when the other boys in the office turned on you. You went to alert your partner and upon returning, the boys had run to their dorm and barricaded themselves in using the metal bunks. You managed to get the door open but they climbed through the window."

"That's right" Frank said.

D.C.I. Smith terminated the interview and walked out of the room with his partner. Detective Constable Nevin.

"What do you think?" She asked.

Smith gave her a puzzled look and said "I think we have to find those boys."

Chapter 9

In the darkness, the boys ran through the muddy fields and eventually stopped to catch their breath when they reach some woodland. They could hear the police and ambulance sirens in the distance but they had run too far to see them.

"Do you think Brian is going to be okay?" Ronnie asked.

"I don't know. I hope they haven't killed him" Mikey said.

"I thought they were going to kill me" Robbo said.

"Yeah, you're lucky me and Alonso reacted when we did."

"Yeah, thanks Ronnie."

"What about Alonso?"

Robbo hesitated for a second.

"Oh, eh thanks."

"No problem, I maybe won't be so quick next time."

"So what did you actually see Mikey?" Matty asked.

"They had him tied to a chair and his face was banged up pretty bad. They were asking about some book. He saw me looking from around the door then Bruce smashed him again in the head with a metal bar."

"It will be the complaints book, they must have found out about it."

"What are we going to do Matty?" Ronnie asked.

"I think we need to find out how Brian is first. If he's okay we have nothing to worry about."

"And if he's not okay."

"Well then we're in a lot of trouble."

"Why? We haven't done anything wrong." Alonso said.

"That's not the way Frank and Bruce will tell it."

"What do you mean? They won't believe them…Will they?"

"No, I'm sure they'll believe six teenage boys with criminal records over two security wardens."

"I never really thought about it like that" Alonso felt worried.

"I think we should keep walking until we can find a place to hide. When the sun comes up we will get to a phone and find out what's happening." Matty stated to let the rest of the boys know he was in charge.

The boys trudged through more muddy fields and headed for a light that they could see in the distance. It was a security light fitted onto the side of a remote farmhouse. There were large sheds and barns close by and Matty led the way as they opened each one to check what was inside. They found one that was stacked with hay and each of them walked in the darkness to the back of the barn. Some of the boys found places to curl up while the others lay back in total silence while staring up at the roof. They all eventually nodded off to sleep. Mikey was woken a few hours later by someone moving around outside the barn. He heard the tractor starting up and driving off. There was a small light coming in through a hole in the roof and Mikey decided to get up and have a look around.

"Where are you going?" Paul whispered.

"I'm just away to check things out and have a look around."

"Good, I'll come with you."

Paul moved quietly so as not to waken the other boys. The sun was rising as they left the barn and they headed straight for the farmer's house.

"Wait Mikey, what if the family are up and about."

"Then we will go back."

They crept around to the back of the house and as Mikey looked in to the kitchen window Paul was opening the back door.

"Can you see anyone?" He whispered to Mikey.

"No."

They entered the kitchen and Paul took out the bread from the bread bin and casually walked over to the fridge.

"There's no butter they've only got margarine." he said as he continued to take out a block of cheese and some ham.

Mikey was busy looking in drawers and cupboards. He looked around and Paul was busy spreading two slices of bread.

"What are you doing?"

"Making myself a sandwich"

"We don't have time for that."

Mikey found what he is looking for, a large carrier bag.

"Put that stuff back in the fridge. Put the bread in this bag and any other loose food that we can all eat."

"What do you mean loose food?"

"Crisps, biscuits or bottles of juice"

"Where are you going?"

"To find a phone"

Mikey walked through the kitchen into the lounge and found a phone near the window.

"Anna. It's Mikey."

"Hi Mikey, what time is it? Is everything okay?"

Brian had helped Mikey track down Anna when he joined The Program and since then; Mikey had visited her weekly and called her every other day.

"It's early Anna. I need a favour, there has been some trouble at The Program and Brian's been hurt. I need you to find out if he's okay."

"What kind of trouble?"

"I saw him being beaten up by the security wardens. They chased us and we think they are going to try and blame it on us. I need you to find out how bad it is."

Mikey heard movement from upstairs.

"I have to go now but I'll call back as soon as I can."

Mikey hung up the phone and made his way back to the kitchen. He found Paul sitting at the table finishing his sandwich and drinking a large glass of milk.

"We have got to go, someone is upstairs" Mikey whispered.

Paul finished his glass of milk and walked over to the sink to wash it.

"What are you doing? Come on."

Mikey can't help but laugh at Paul who was more concerned about cleaning up after himself than being caught in someone's house. He picked up the carrier bag and they quietly walked out of the back door and back to the barn.

"Hey guys, we have your breakfast" Paul said waking the rest of the boys.

"Where did this come from?" Matty asked while Paul emptied the bag.

"From the house just outside" Mikey said.

"That's good, did you not think of telling us you were going?" He said sternly.

"You were all sleeping, what's the problem?"

"Because we don't know what's going on with Brian and when the farmer realises his house has been broken into there will be police all over here."

"Don't worry about it, we didn't break in. The door was open and any mess we made, Paul cleaned it up. Actually the place is probably cleaner now than be-fore we went in" Mikey looked at Paul and they both laughed.

Matty squared up to Mikey.

"Do you think this is funny?"

Mikey's smile dropped. Ronnie stepped forward and wedged himself in between them.

"Come on guys, the last thing we need is to be fighting amongst ourselves. Let us eat this and we will go and find out what the story is with Brian."

"Yeah, come on guys" Alonso said as he stood up and pulled on Mikey's arm to sit down.

"In Brian's absence, I'm in charge and I make the decisions" Matty demanded.

"We know mate, just sit down and forget it."

Matty sat down and Robbo passed him some bread.

"Mikey you know whenever Brian left the camp, he always left someone in charge, and he nominated Matty" Ronnie informed him.

Mikey didn't say anything but shrugged his shoulders and picked up a piece of bread.

The boys polished off most of the stolen food and Matty decided that it was not safe to stay in the barn. He led the way back through the same muddy fields that they hiked through the night before. As the got closer to the camp they took a different route and walked towards Dundee.

"I'm hungry again" Ronnie said.

"You're always hungry" Robbo replied.

"But we have been walking for ages now and I've worked up an appetite. I need some food."

"Look there's a shop up ahead." Robbo said as he pointed to small local convenience store.

"Does anyone have any money?" Matty said.

"No. But a small shop like that has got to be run by Pakis, Alonso will be related, so he can get us sorted out" Robbo said

"No we're not all related because were not all Paki-stani's. My parents are Chilean. And even if I was related, and you were dying of hunger you're the last person I would go and get food for."

"Ah don't you two start again. Look if we can get to a phone I will find out about Brian, then if it's safe, we can all head back to the camp" Matty said.

"You guys can look for a phone. I'm going for some food" Ronnie said before storming off in the direction of the shop.

"I'm with Ronnie, and besides, the Paki will probably have a phone anyway." Robbo said as he ran off before Alonso could say anything back to him.

The others looked at Matty.

"We should head for the shop. They'll probably have a phone there. Come on guys" Matty said in an attempt to save face as the leader.

The boys looked at each other and smiled as they knew Matty's role as leader had just been tested. The boys walked into the shop together and separated as they went down the small isles.

"I told you it was a Paki shop." Robbo whispered to Alonso before ducking under a shelf.

"It's Pakistani not Paki" Alonso said angrily.

Matty approached the shop owner who stood nerv-ously behind the counter. He politely asked if he could use his telephone. The shop owner looked him up and down and then scanned the shop for the rest of the boys.

"You boys are in real trouble." He said

"What do you mean?"

The owner didn't answer. He marched out from be-hind the counter and down the aisle. He grabbed Robbo by the arm and pulled out a packet of biscuits from under his t-shirt.

"Get out of my shop you little thieves, the lot of you. Get out."

Ronnie looked over at the freezer.

"Look guys choc ices" He said as he opened the lid and took one out.

"Put it back" The owner shouted.

Ronnie threw one across the shop to Paul who opened the wrapper and bit into it.

"Mmm, not bad"

"Guys what are you doing, Brian will go nuts" Matty pleaded.

The boys ran around the shop while the owner chased them and tried to throw them out. While all this commotion was going on, Mikey sneaked behind the counter and picked up the phone. He quickly dialled Anna's number.

"It's Mikey. I only have a few seconds. What's the news on Brian?"

"Oh Mikey it's been on the radio all morning. Brian has been murdered and the police say they are looking for six teenage boys in connection with it. Mikey I..."

The line went dead.

"Get out of my shop" The owner said as he peered over the counter to Mikey who was crouched on the floor.

He had pulled the plug out of the phone. Mikey put the receiver down and sat for a few seconds taking in the news. He stood up and looked at Ronnie who had a carrier bag in one hand and was filling it with the other. They locked eyes and Mikey shook his head slightly. Ronnie knew straight away that something was wrong.

"Is it Brian?"

Mikey nodded

"Is he dead?"

Mikey nodded again. Ronnie let go of the bag and his eyes widened. The owner grabbed Ronnie and pushed him towards the door.

"Get out, get out" He shouted.

Ronnie turned and pushed the owner back. The owner grabbed Ronnie and put him in a head lock. They stumbled around the shop knocking over shelves and display stalls before Ronnie fell to his knees. The owner tightened his grip and Ronnie was about to pass out when Mikey picked up a bottle of beer from behind the counter and ran towards them. He smashed it over the owners head and he released his grip from around Ronnie's neck.

"Come on, we've got to get out of here" Matty shouted.

The boys ran to the door but Ronnie was still on the floor coughing and struggling to regain his breathing. Mikey held the door open to wait on Ronnie. He struggled to his feet and took a few steps towards the door before he turned back to pick up the bag of food. Mikey shook his head and smiled.

Chapter 10

The boys ran through a large part of waste ground until they reached a small wooded area. Matty, who was leading the way, stopped once he thought they were in deep enough that passers-by wouldn't see them. Ronnie passed around the bag of stolen food.

"Are you not having any Ronnie?" Paul asked.

"Nah, I'm not really hungry anymore."

"Why what's wrong?"

Ronnie looked at Mikey and nodded at him to tell them.

"What's going on?" Paul looked at Mikey.

"I have something to tell you" Mikey said.

"We kind of gathered that, what is it?"

"It's about Brian."

They all stopped eating and looked at Mikey, they knew they were are about to hear bad news.

"He's dead. They killed him."

The boys all stared at each other and shook their heads in disbelief.

"How did you find out?" Matty asked.

"I made a call from the shop."

"Who did you call?"

"My foster mother, she said it's been on the radio all morning and the police are looking for six teenage boys."

"What, they think we did it?" Alonso asked.

"She never said. She just said she we are wanted in connection with it."

"Of course they think we did it. Frank and Bruce are not exactly going to admit that they did it are they" Robbo said.

"I don't feel hungry anymore either" Alonso threw the food on the ground.

"So where do we go from here?" Robbo asked.

The boys in turn, all looked at Matty."

"Why are you all looking at me?"

"Because you're our nominated leader, remember?" Mikey said.

Matty paused for a minute.

"I guess we go back and explain what happened. Let them know the truth."

The boys sat in silence for a long time as they thought about the prospect of going back to face Frank and Bruce and also the thought of being sent back to the Institution.

"You know they're never going to believe us don't you" Mikey said.

"Well what do you suggest we do?" Matty asked. He hated that Mikey had said what was on everyone's mind.

"Find Scott, he'll know what to do."

"Yeah, Scott will help us. That sounds good to me. Yeah let's go find Scott" Robbo said.

The boys' faces lit up and they looked at Matty for his decision.

"And how are we supposed to find him. We don't even know where he lives."

"I do" Ronnie said.

The boys all looked at Ronnie.

"And how do you know that?"

"Brian left me in his office once, it was a while back and I read some files. I remembered Scott's address because it wasn't too far from where I used to live."

"If it was a while ago what's to say he hasn't moved since then?"

"What's to say he has?" Mikey quickly replied.

"Come on Matty, it's our only hope. Unless you want to go back and face being charged with Brian's murder" Robbo said.

Matty didn't take long to think about this as he looked at the faces staring at him. He realised that if he decided to hand himself in, he would be doing it alone.

"Right we'll go, but we'll have to wait here until it gets dark. I don't think it would be wise for us to walk about in broad daylight if they are looking for six teenage boys."

***

"What do you mean you couldn't find the book?" Williamson shouted as Frank and Bruce stood rooted to the spot in his office. Both of them felt like schoolboys receiving a telling off from their teacher.

"Barney...eh Councillor Williamson, we turned that office upside down. There was no way he wouldn't tell us after the beating we gave him." Frank pleaded.

"Who else had access to that office?"

"No one"

"What about Scott?"

Frank and Bruce looked at each other and back to Williamson.

"I think you two had better get around there before that book ends up in the wrong hands" Williamson threatened.

Both men walked towards the door and as Bruce opened it, he had one foot touching the marbled floor in the reception area when Williamson shouted

"You had better get that book. Whatever it takes"

Williamson's ranting was nothing new to the council staff in the building that overheard him. His loud and threatening behaviour had become the norm to most of the staff that they never paid much attention to it. Rosie, one of his assistants, was by her desk trying to look busy, but she had taken in every word. She knew exactly what book he was referring to as it had been handed to her the night before. As the two employees in their security uniforms walked past her desk, her heart skipped a beat. She knew where they were heading and she knew she had to get out of the office to make a phone call. If she used the phone from her desk it could be traced back to her. She watched as the two men entered the lift and the doors closed. After gathering some papers together, she casually walked over and pressed the button on the lift. She flicked through the papers in her arm as though they were important documents and glanced at the numbers up above as they went to zero and slowly come back up to four. She entered the lift and as soon as the door opened on the bottom floor she walked as fast as she could to the nearest phone box. Her hands were shaking as she dialled the number...no answer. She dialled again...no answer. Where could he be? Hopefully he won't be home until after they've been. She had heard Williamson loud and clear. His two goons were told 'whatever it takes.' She knew that meant

Scott could be hurt. Scott had never hurt anybody in his life. There wasn't a bad bone in his body. When he got out of the army and came to his sister for a job, she didn't hesitate to pull some strings to help him. He was her kid brother. She had been married and divorced but having kept her married name, no one knew they were related. She knew he would be great with those kids but at the same time she was using him to keep her informed about The Program. In a way she felt she was no better than Williamson. If anything happened to Scott, it would be on her conscience. What was worrying her now was that Scott could tell them who he passed the book to. She hung up the receiver and quickly walked to the car park. She was soon speeding out of the city centre towards Scott's house.

There was a car parked outside when she arrived so she pulled up further along the street and waited. Several minutes later Scott's front door opened and Frank and Bruce walked out. She pulled out a note pad from her handbag and recorded the time. After they sped off out of the street she got out of her car and walked quickly towards Scott's house, hoping and praying that he wasn't home. The front door appeared to be unlocked but after a closer inspection she noticed it had been burst open.

"Scott, are you home?" She shouted as she entered the hallway.

A quick glance into the living room revealed that the place had been turned over. Her heart was beating fast and her legs began to shake as she walked up the stairs.

"Scott. Scott" She shouted.

She slowly opened his bedroom door to find him lying face down on his bed. Her worst fear had come true. She leaned over him and turned his head to the side. She put her hand to her mouth in shock and was close to vomiting. There was a thin red line going around his neck revealing to her that he had been strangled. There were also finger marks where it looked as though he had tried to release whatever material they used. She felt for a pulse…nothing.

She hurried out of the house and back to her car. She only drove a short distance and had to stop. Her stomach started to retch and she opened her door to vomit. She hadn't eaten today so the retching brought nothing up. Her eyes bulged and the tears were flowing as she made her way home. She wanted to go to the police but that would mean giving a statement against Williamson and handing over all the evidence she had gathered. She felt that she was not ready to do that yet. She didn't know who to trust as Williamson had bought over so many people. She took a deep breath and drove to a friend's house. Bernice had been her friend since they were young and was the only person that she trusted.

"What's wrong? What's happened?" Bernice said upon seeing her friend in such a distressed state.

She ushered her inside and once she had calmed down she explained to her what had happened. Bernice went straight outside and opened her garage doors, she drove Rosie's car inside to hide it, in case they come looking for her. Bernice arranged for her husband to go to Rosie's home and collect some of her things, she warned him to make sure he was not followed. Rosie wanted to report the murder but Bernice persuaded her that they should leave it until later in the hope that someone else discovered it. If they didn't hear anything by nine that night, she would drive to a phone box at the other end of town and make an anonymous call. It was now a waiting game for Rosie. She had the evidence against Williamson but if he was capable of arranging a murder, she was also in danger. As soon as Scott's body was discovered Williamson would find out that they were related.

***

It began to get dark around eight o' clock and Matty noticed the rest of the boys were beginning to get restless.

"Come on Matty. What are we waiting on?" Robbo asked.

"Yeah Matty, if we leave it too late it will look even more suspicious if the six of us are wandering around at night" Ronnie said.

Matty started to think about this and made a decision.

"Okay let's go. Ronnie you lead the way as you're the only one who knows where he lives."

Ronnie walked off with Mikey and Paul at either side of him. He took the quiet back streets whenever possible and hid if anything resembled a police car. Upon reaching Scott's street, Ronnie led them down a dark path that ran parallel with the back gardens. Ronnie stopped halfway down the path and told the rest of the boys to wait.

"Where are you going?" Matty asked.

"I have to find out which one is Scott's."

Ronnie climbed a fence and walked to the front of the house. He was at number seven and Scott's was eleven.

"Two doors down guys"

The boys made their way over Scott's fence and Matty was in front as they approached Scott's front door.

"It doesn't look as though he is in. There's no light on."

"Just knock anyway." Ronnie said.

Matty knocked on the door and it slid open.

"Guys the doors open."

"Go in then."

"I'm not away to walk into his house."

"Paul." Ronnie whispered loudly.

Paul casually walked up the steps and into the house switching the lights on as he passed them.

"His place is a bit of a tip. Does Scott never clean up after himself?" Paul commented on seeing the living room.

"It looks as though he's been doing a bit of decorating" Robbo said sarcastically.

"Somehow I don't think this is Scott's mess" Mikey said

"Scott. Scott, are you in? We need your help" Ronnie shouted.

"It's starting to look more like he may need our help" Robbo said.

Ronnie made his way up the stairs.

"Scott, its Ronnie, we need your help."

He opened the bedroom door and put the light on. He jumped back when he saw Scott's body lying on the bed.

"What? What is it?" Robbo asked.

"Scott. Scott, wake up" Ronnie shouted.

"Somehow I don't think Scott's sleeping" Robbo said.

"Will you shut up?"

Ronnie walked forward and touched his neck to feel for a pulse. He knew by how cold he was that Scott was dead.

"He's freezing, and guys, check out those marks on his neck."

"I'm guessing we can rule out Scott helping us then" Robbo said.

Mikey looked at Robbo and shook his head. He picked up a sheet and pulled it up to cover Scott's body.

"What do you think happened?" Alonso asked.

"Well he didn't strangle himself did he?" Robbo said.

"But why would...?" Alonso stopped mid-sentence as Mikey put his finger to his lips.

"Shhh, guys be quiet."

In the distance they could hear police sirens and they began to get louder.

"Come on. We have to get out of here."

The boys rushed down the stairs and as they reached the front door they could see the blue flashing lights speeding up the street. The first police car screeched to a halt in the street and the officers caught sight of the boys as they ran around the side of the house. The officer in the passenger seat was quick off the mark to give chase. As he ran after them he took out his torch in one hand and his truncheon in the other. He caught up with the boys as they were midway through climbing the back fence. The officer lifted up his arm holding the truncheon as he approached Alonso and brought it down hard on the top of his head. Alonso crashed to the ground on the opposite side of the fence. The officer placed his truncheon back into his utility belt and started to climb the fence but Mikey smacked him in the face with a shovel. It startled him but he kept coming. Mikey hit him again and he fell back down the same side. Mikey dropped the shovel and grabbed hold of Alonso's arm.

"Come on. Run."

Alonso was dragged to his feet and pulled up the path by Mikey. They were out of sight by the time the other officers arrived. Ronnie grew up in the same area and knew it like the back of his hand. He led them through many gardens and out onto the main road.

"We can't go on the main road Ronnie. They'll be driving up here any minute" Matty said.

"Look I know what I'm doing, trust me. They will have the dogs out so we'll have to shake off our scent."

Ronnie knew exactly where he was heading. The law, a large hill located close to the middle of the city. It is 174 metres above sea level and the base is surrounded by thick woodland. From the housing area around the bottom, there is a road that winds through the trees until it reaches its summit. This attracts the tourists as they view the whole city and beyond from each angle. At night, the woodland surrounding the hill is in complete darkness.

Ronnie crossed the main road which took them to two streets with rows of tenements. He ordered them to split up and run through the front of the tenements and out the back all the way along the street.

"If you see a wall, climb it. We will meet at the other end."

The boys did exactly as Ronnie said and crossed each other's paths as they ran to confuse the dogs. They carried on up the street and climbed the large wall at the end.

"Right guys follow me" Ronnie said.

"I don't think I can run anymore" Paul lifted up his chest to help him take in more air to his lungs.

"It's okay it's not far."

"Why are you so unfit Paul? Is that because you used to smoke?" Alonso asked.

"I never smoked. I only said that when I was caught with matches or a lighter."

Ronnie ran across the main road towards the thick tree at the base of The Law. He had been through here many times in the dark when he ran away as a young boy and knew every path and where it led to. They came to a large wire fence surrounding an area of allotments and Ronnie was about to climb the fence when he realised the amount of footprints they would leave. He walked around to the other side of the allotments and climbed over. With the others not far behind, he made his way to a small shed and placed his hand under the gap in the door.

"It's been a long time. My hands are nearly too big to fit through the gap."

He slid out a key and unlocked the door.

"Whose place is this?" Matty asked.

"It's an old guy who lives near here. He knew the trouble I was in at home and said if I needed a place to go…well I guess he still leaves the key for me."

Chapter 11

A full scale search for the boys went on through the night until the early hours of the morning. Officers from other areas were drafted in to help with the door to door enquiries. The police began to think that the boys were hiding in one of the tenement flats as this was where the dogs began to lose their scent.

Smith was tired but decided to go back to his office before going home for some much needed sleep. He had a message on his desk that Scott's time of death was approximately two in the afternoon.

'Surely the boys would not have hung around all that time' Smith thought. 'The call to the police station to inform them about the murder was from a woman and was made from a phone box five miles away. Whoever made that call had to have been there to know that Scott was already dead. If she saw the boys kill him, why did she go five miles away to make the call?' Smith tried hard to piece it together but the continuous thought gave him a headache.

He began to prepare his statement for the press when a folder that had recently been placed on his desk, attracted his attention. It was nearly an inch thick and had a post-it attached.

FAO
D.C.I. Smith

When he opened the folder, he was faced with pho-tos of all six boys. It was their files and background reports. He flicked through each of them and one photo stood out more than the others. Michael McDonnell. He picked up the photo and stared at it. He knew the name well, and the photo looked very familiar to him. He took out the boys file and started to read.

'Taken into care at the age of four after both parents were killed in a car crash...Father - William McDonnell...Brother William McDonnell...'

"William. Holy shit, he's Billy's baby brother" He mumbled to himself.

Smith sat back in his chair but kept his eyes focused on the folder lying open in front of him. He stared at the photo of Mikey and how much he resembled Billy and their Father. Smith started to think about the past when he was still a struggling detective.

The McDonnell's had arrived in Dundee from the province of Northern Ireland. Billy, his pregnant wife and their young son, also named Billy, had come over to escape the troubles. Billy senior had spent time in The Maze, also known as Long Kesh prison. In the time that he had been inside, his own teenage son had become involved in the troubles. Upon his release he tried hard to guide him away from it, but the violence and loss was in their faces every day, and to Billy Senior, it was a losing battle. He was worried for his son as he knew that one day he would end up like himself, in prison, or worse, he would end up dead. He had witnessed many of his friends lose their close relatives and when his wife announced she was pregnant again, he decided it was time to move away.

It was not long after arriving in Dundee that Billy's wife gave birth to another son, Michael, and it was around this time that Smith first came across Young Billy. He had found it hard to settle after knowing only violence and crime his whole life. One night, as Smith was given the task of taking Young Billy back home after having been picked up for a minor crime, he was taken aback by the hostility he received from both the boy and his father and the hatred they had for the police. It had come to the point where officers avoided arresting Young Billy so as they did not have to face his father. Each time there was an incident involving Young Billy, the officer dealing with the case noted him as Billy's kid. After several appearances at the children's panel Billy's parents were informed that there were only so many excuses they could make for Young Billy and the next time he appeared they would consider the possibility of placing him into Borstal. This settled Young Billy down and he managed to avoid getting himself into trouble for a while. Billy's parents occasionally travelled back to Ireland to visit relatives and with Billy's progress they thought it best that he stayed here. They did not want him to be mixing with his old friends and reverting back to his old ways. It was during one of their parent's visits back home, while Mikey and Billy were being looked after by family friends Charlie and Anna, that Young Billy received the phone call. It was the devastating news that their parents had been killed in a car crash. Charlie and Anna stuck by Young Billy and travelled back with him to bury his parents. They were given foster care of Mikey and asked Young Billy to come back with them as this is what his parents would have wanted. Billy felt as though he had nothing and soon reverted back to his old ways of violence and crime. Only this time, Billy was no longer a minor and his crimes were becoming more serious. He had grown wise to the authorities and with the help of his close circle of loyal friends they were finding it harder to catch him. With Billy senior now gone, he was no longer Billy's kid, and the authorities were now labelling him as Billy the Kid due to his notorious behaviour. The police had little evidence but they knew Billy and his crew were behind several burglaries that had occurred in the city. Smith, who was put in charge of the case, had picked up one of Billy's circle of friends, one who liked to talk. Every move Billy made, Smith was onto him. The police were closing in and Billy knew it was only a matter of time before he was caught. He made a decision, he had to leave.

Smith looked over at the press statement that he had started to write and suddenly an idea came into his head. He had his doubts from the start about the murder of Brian and he knew exactly which leads he should have been following up, but he had waited a long time for an opportunity like this. The whole situation could give him the chance to catch Billy's kid. He now felt wide awake and pulled his chair closer to his desk. He ripped up the original statement and started again.

***

The boys had been hiding out in the shed for two days now. Ronnie had left early each morning with Matty and brought back rolls, milk and newspapers for the rest of the boys. From the top of The Law, they had watched the deliveries being made and quickly swooped down to help themselves. On the third morning Mikey had watched through a small window in the roof of the shed and had noticed that the night sky was starting to clear. He had lain awake for hours and like the other boys, had become restless. He nudged Ronnie who was sound asleep and snoring away. Ronnie was reluctant to move until Mikey mentioned that if they did not go for food now they would have to wait until tomorrow. Ronnie was soon on his feet, stretching and ready to go. They walked to the top of The Law and looked down on the empty streets below. They could see the top of the police incident box at the end of Scott's street. No doubt it contained some bored officers being paid to sit in there and drink coffee all night. They watched the same milk float as yesterday doing its deliveries and Mikey stood up to make his move.

"Not this one" Ronnie said and shook his head.

"Why not"

"We did that one yesterday"

"So?"

"If it's a one off they won't take any notice but if their deliveries are short two days in a row, they will look into it"

"I take it you've did this a lot?"

Ronnie didn't answer but gave him a smile.

They didn't have to wait long before another milk float appeared in an area to the left of them down below. They took their time walking down the hill, taking extra care to stick to the thick bushes wherever possible. When they reached the streets below, they casually walked to the local shop and helped themselves to rolls and newspapers that had been delivered less than an hour before. On the way back up the hill they took a detour to the area where the milk had been delivered and picked up cartons of milk from random doorsteps before heading back to the shed.

Paul was the first to open up one of the newspapers as he munched on a roll.

"Mikey"

"Yeah, what is it?"

"I think you had better take a look at this"

Paul turned the paper around and the rest of the boys squeezed together to read under the small light from the roof window. The story was a double paged spread about Mikey's brother with a large photo of him from when he was younger.

"He looks just like you Mikey" Robbo commented.

"Why? What does it say?" Alonso asked.

"Oh I forgot. Do you need it translated?" Robbo said.

"No I just can't see for your big head."

Mikey looked up and stared at them and they both tilted their heads to keep reading.

"It says here that Mikey's brother Billy is still wanted in connection with a few armed robberies from over ten years ago" Ronnie said.

"What else?" Alonso asked.

Ronnie scanned down the page.

"'Billy's brother Mikey is the leader of the gang of runaways who are now wanted in connection with two murders'...that means they think we killed Scott as well."

"Gang, they think we're a gang now, and Mikey's our leader" Robbo said.

"Yeah but look at the photo of Mikey."

"That's me?" Matty said.

Mikey took the paper and stared at the photo of his brother before reading the article over again. He thought about what his brother must have been like back then and tried to imagine what he would do in his situation.

"Guys, seriously, I think we should hand ourselves in now. This has gotten way out of hand" Matty pleaded.

"I'm not handing myself in. I've done nothing wrong" Alonso said.

"All the more reason for us to go back and tell them it wasn't us. We wouldn't even be in this situation if it wasn't for you Mikey" Matty said.

"What's that supposed to mean?" Mikey looked up from the paper.

"Well it was your idea to go to Scott's house. If we hadn't gone there, we wouldn't be in this mess."

Mikey snapped back "So it's all fault for walking in on Frank and Bruce when they had Brian tied to his chair while they beat him to death."

"Are you sure it wasn't you that did it? And maybe they walked in on you."

Mikey dropped the paper and dived on Matty. He managed to land a fist to the side of his face before they both ended up wrestling on the floor. Mikey managed to get on top and threw several more punches to Matty's head.

Ronnie pulled Mikey off and the rest of the boys held Matty back.

"You're just as much to blame for this as me. I never asked you to come here. I never asked you to come to Scott's house either. If you want to go and hand yourself in, none of us will stop you, off you go" Mikey shouted.

"Guys, guys, no-one here is to blame. We're all in this together."

Mikey and Matty sat back and nothing was said be-tween the two. The rest of the boys also sat in silence as they contemplated their options. Mikey passed the paper to Alonso, who had been waiting patiently to read the story, he thought of a plan but knew it was not the right time to bring it up. He decided to keep quiet and see how things turned out.

***

Smith had been in the office all morning looking over the notes from all the unconfirmed sightings of the boys from the last two days. He was about to leave for lunch and picked up his jacket when D.C. Nevin appeared with a large map in her hand. She spread it across his desk. Three areas were circled in pencil. Smith recognised one of the areas as Scott's street.

"What are these?" he said pointing to the two other circles.

"We've received a report from a shop in the glens area. There was a quantity of rolls stolen early this morning and residents have complained about their milk not being delivered when the dairy was adamant that they delivered it. The two detectives stood and stared at the map laid out in front of them. Ronnie had specifically chosen to steal from different areas so as not to alert suspicion but Nevin was looking at it in exactly the same way. She tried to place herself in certain locations where the boys could be hiding and would be able to obtain access to all of the areas circled. She mentioned to Smith the different locations and put together scenarios of why the boys would be in those particular places. Smith stood and stared at the map for a long time.

"I think we are looking too much at the bigger picture."

"What do you mean?"

"Well if I send out teams of officers to all these locations that you mention it will use up all our re-sources. If the boys see the large police presence they will be less likely to come out of hiding or it could even make them move further away. I believe they are a lot closer than we think. Another day won't hurt, wait until tomorrow and if more deliveries go missing we could narrow the area down further. Have extra officers on stand-by for tomorrow morning and as soon as the report comes in, we will make our move."

Nevin picked up the map and walked out of the office. Smith followed her as far as the stair landing and then turned towards the lift. He knew if this worked out, the boys, or at least some of the boys, would be in custody by this time tomorrow. This was not what he had planned but he knew he had to appear genuine enough about catching the boys. If any of his superiors knew his intentions he would be sacked on the spot.

***

Davie 'Buster' McNaughton had only recently been released from prison and was catching up with a few acquaintances in his local haunt, The Claverhouse. As he sat by the bar, a newspaper that a customer had left behind caught his eye. It was neither the headline nor the story that interested him as he had never been one for current affairs. It was the accompanying photo of D.C.I. Smith, the same detective that had assisted in his prison stretch. The story accompanying the photo was of the teenage boys wanted for murder, which was now, a major topic of conversation. When he opened the newspaper, he, unexpectedly, saw an old friend staring back at him, intrigued at his connection to the story, he read on. 'Billy McDonnell, brother of Michael McDonnell....' Buster quickly finished his drink and folded the newspaper under his arm. It was time to visit Murdoch.

Buster walked into the Pheasant pub and received a few strange looks by the regular patrons. Each one of them knew him, and his troublesome reputation, so were somewhat sceptical of his appearance in their local bar.

"Are you lost or something pal?" A voice piped up not too far from him.

Buster turned swiftly and broke into a smile. "Kevin."

Kevin stood up and shook his hand and the punters in the bar relaxed. Buster took up a seat and placed the newspaper from under his arm on the bar in front of Kevin.

"Did you learn to read when you were inside?" He joked.

"I take it you've read about these young lads on the run for murder?"

"Of course, I've not paid too much attention to it but I would gladly assist them in any way I can, they have been quite beneficial to me."

"How come"

"Well, they are using up all the police resources so I have basically had carte blanche to, let's say, carry out some of my activities" He winked.

"Turn to page five" Buster nodded.

Kevin slid the newspaper closer and flicked the pag-es. He raised his eyebrows when he saw the old mug shot of Billy.

"Now look at the kids name in the photo next to him."

"Michael McDonnell. Ooh, this is not good."

"Are you still in touch with Billy?"

"I have a number."

"I think it's maybe best that you give him a call."

Buster stood up to leave. "Oh, and eh, it's probably best you tell him that Smith is in charge of the case."

***

Billy had been hard at work sanding the crumbling paint from the underside of a small boat when he felt a tap on his shoulder. It was Nina, Billy's girlfriend of several years. When Billy left Scotland he travelled around for a long time and worked various jobs to pay his way. He had met Nina in a bar one night and she mentioned that her grandfather was looking for a hand cleaning up old boats by the beach. He died several years ago but Billy had learned enough from him to manage the place on his own. Nina dealt with the business side of things.

"Yeah, what is it?" He said lifting up his dust mask.

"You have a phone call."

"Who is it?"

"I don't know. I couldn't really understand him he talked very fast. He asked for Billy the kid."

Billy smiled upon hearing this as he knew there was only one person from back home who had his number.

"Hello."

"Is this Billy's kid?" He said putting on a posh voice.

"Kevin Murdoch, how's it going? Let me guess, you've heard some gossip that you just have to tell some-one."

"Nah, nothing like that, I wondered if you received our newspapers out there"

"Yeah, they're usually a day or two late but yeah. Why?"

"There is a group of youngsters from Dundee on the run for a murder. Well actually, it says here they are now wanted in connection with two murders"

Billy is about to ask the obvious question but feels he already knows the answer.

"Mikey" he blurted out.

"They've been on the run for a few days now, I would have called sooner but it's only just been brought to my attention."

"What does the article say?"

"A group of kids from a boy's home are wanted in connection with the murder of Brian Malliff, a social worker that ran the secure unit where the boys were being supervised. Two days ago a warden who also worked there was found dead in his home. As I said, I never really paid much attention to it until the name came up. I've put the word out, as soon as I hear anything I'll get back to you."

"Okay be quick."

"Will do Billy"

Billy put the receiver down and stared at the wall.

"What wrong Billy?" Nina asked. She sensed that it was bad news.

"It's my kid brother. He's in a lot of trouble. I think I'll have to go back and help him."

"I thought you said you could never go back."

"I can't, but my brother needs my help...Nina could you try and get hold of some British newspapers, the later the edition, the better."

"Where are you going?"

"I'll have to go and use up a few favours that I am due."

Chapter 12

It was the third night the boys had stayed in the shed and each one was becoming restless. Ronnie didn't mind it so much as he had stayed there on many occasions when there was trouble at home. There was the constant feeling of hunger and this resulted in petty arguments that escalated to Ronnie having to step in before they came to blows. None of the boys had slept much on that third night and it was still dark when Ronnie announced that he was going for a walk up the hill. The other boys decided to go with him. As they sat at the top of the Law looking down on the whole of the city, the sky started to became clearer. Paul commented on deliveries being made to a shop down below that they had not ventured near.

"That shop is only one street away from Scott's house" Ronnie said.

"So?"

"Do you see that white box lit up down there? That's full of police waiting to catch us."

"Exactly, that is the last place they would expect us to go" Paul said.

There was silence for a few seconds as all the boys looked down.

"He's right you know" Mikey said.

The boys all looked at each other.

"Come on, let's go. My stomach has been rumbling all night" Robbo said.

When they reached the bottom of the hill, the boys split up. Ronnie, Matty and Alonso made their way to the shop to steal the rolls and Mikey, Robbo and Paul went in search of milk. On approaching the street with the police incident box, Robbo noticed cartons of milk on the doorstep opposite.

"Paul" Robbo nudged him and nodded in the direction of the milk.

Paul smiled back and swaggered out from the bushes where they were hiding.

"Don't be stupid" Mikey said.

Paul looked back with a large grin as he exaggerated his swagger. Upon reaching the police box, he walked confidently around it to reach the garden opposite. He picked up two cartons of milk and while passing the incident box on his return he did a little dance before hurrying back to the bushes.

"You're not right mate" Robbo laughed.

On the way back to meet the others they walked through a side street and picked up some more car-tons of milk. Robbo also managed to take some newspapers back out of their letter boxes.

They made their way back up the Law and sat stuffing their faces with the freshly made rolls. Robbo opened one of the newspapers and nudged Matty.

"What is it?"

Robbo nodded at the story in the paper and both boys looked at each other.

"Ronnie."

"Yeah, what is it?"

Neither boy said a word but stared back at Ronnie. He looked at the page and took the paper from Robbo. Ronnie's smile soon dropped from his face as he looked on in disgust at a photo of his father in a wheelchair with his mother by his side. Above the photo was the heading 'This is what my son, the killer, did to me.' The story went on to say how Ronnie used to beat up his father on a regular basis and one day he went too far. Now his father needs twenty four hour care. Ronnie sat down and read the full story then looked up to see all the boys crowded around him. He knew that even if the story were true, not one of these boys would judge him. They all had a past and they were all picked by Brian for the same reason. Although feeling hurt and angry, Ronnie looked at the other boys and smiled. He now realised the extent in which Brian's influence had on them. Ronnie glanced back at the newspaper and one word stood out to him, it was part of the heading that said 'Killer.' This gave Ronnie somewhat of a reality check.

"Guys they've called me a killer"

Mikey laughed "I wouldn't take it personally Ronnie."

"No, but you don't understand. Some people will actually believe this shit"

"Ronnie we're all in this together mate" Robbo said.

Ronnie threw the paper aside and watched as it soaks up the wet from the ground.

"Good one Ronnie. How are the rest of us supposed to read it now?" Alonso said.

"What do you mean? You can't read anyway, it's in English" Robbo said.

"Guys I think we should get back to the shed before we're seen" Matty said.

"Is there nowhere else we can go to hide out, I really don't want to be stuck in there all day again" Paul said.

Ronnie walked off in the direction of the shed and the boys followed with Robbo and Alonso trying to trip each other up as they walked.

"Shh" Mikey said as he stopped suddenly.

"What is it?" Ronnie whispered.

"Look, over there" he said pointing through the trees.

The boys looked to see several police officers with torches at the foot of the Law. Robbo was too interested in tripping up Alonso to notice what was going on and laughed out loud when Alonso went head first down a small mud slide. The rest of the boys gave Robbo a stern look. They watched as the torches began moving in their direction. For all the abuse Robbo had given Alonso, he was the first one down the hill to help him. The boys moved quickly through the trees and with Mikey out in front, he led them to the base of the Law, stopping short of the road.

"Where do we go now Ronnie?"

Ronnie made a quick decision. He knew it would lead to more trouble but after reading the lies in the newspaper, now was good a time as any to see what they had to say for themselves.

"Follow me." He said.

Ronnie ran across the main road and climbed a fence into someone's back garden. He kept on running until he reached his destination. He opened the back door to a tenement block and waited inside for the others to catch up.

"Where are we?" Mikey asked as he caught his breath.

Ronnie didn't answer but nodded to a door behind him. Mikey looked at the name plate.

"Martin. Are you sure this is a good idea Ronnie?"

Ronnie shrugged his shoulders. "Where else are we going to go?"

"What are we waiting here for?" Robbo asked.

They all looked at Ronnie for an answer. He turned to face the door and hesitated for a few seconds. He signalled for the others to stand away from the door out of sight. With his stomach in knots he knocked on the door lightly. No answer. He clattered the letter box and waited anxiously.

"Who is it?" A voice behind the door asked.

"It's Tayside Police" He said in a deep voice.

His mother opened the door and a familiar smell wafted from inside the house, it was a rancid smell of dirty smoke and stale alcohol. Ronnie's Mother stared at him for a few seconds before she recognised who it was. He had grown in height and filled out considerably. After years of malnutrition he was now a muscular and clean cut young man. Although sleeping rough the last few days hadn't helped much.

"Ronnie. What are you doing here?" She sounded distraught.

"Yeah it's good to see you too mum" He said sarcastically.

"What do you want?"

"My friends and I need a place to hang out for a bit"

"So you come crawling back here after everything you have put us through" She said in her hoarse voice.

"I knew this was a bad idea" Ronnie mumbled.

He turned on his heels to walk away and caught sight of the other boys faces staring back at him. They looked tired, dirty and cold. He turned back once more and caught his foot in the door as his mother tried to close it. He pushed the door wide open and nudged her out of the way.

"Mum these are my friends and we're going to be staying for a bit. Come on in lads" He marched through the house and the other boys trailed behind him.

Ronnie opened the living room door and the foul smell hit him full on. The dark room was littered with empty tins and bottles. Ronnie's father sat in a drunken stupor in his wheelchair in front of the television. His mother had been too drunk the night before to put him to his bed. The boys looked on from the doorway as Ronnie cleared the couch and chairs of rubbish.

"Grab a seat guys. I'll put the kettle on"

Ronnie walked into the kitchen to find his mother pouring herself a drink.

"Now, there's a familiar scene."

He opened the fridge to find a full crate of cheap lager.

"Where are you going with them, they're your uncle Jimmy's"

"Where is he?"

"He's asleep in your old room."

Ronnie smiled "How convenient, well, I'm sure he won't mind."

Ronnie feared his uncle Jimmy as much as his father when he was growing up. He had subjected him to as much, if not more, physical abuse than his father had. Ronnie walked into the living room where the boys had gathered around the television, they were waiting patiently on the local morning news.

"Help yourselves guys."

The boys' eyes lit up at the thought of being offered alcohol. They all leaned forward and took a tin, all except Alonso.

"Is that beer? I don't drink beer?" Alonso said.

"Get it down you, you wimp" Robbo said.

Alonso felt the peer pressure and reluctantly opened a tin and sipped from it.

"That's disgusting."

The boys all laughed

"Just keep drinking. You'll get used to it. The first taste is always like that" Paul said.

"Yeah and before you know it, you'll be living in a shit hole like this and be drinking the stuff for breakfast" Ronnie said.

He shouted on his mother who was busy in the kitchen topping up her drink. He told her to make up some food. His father began to stir from his slumber and realising his son was in the house, he shouted on Ronnie's mother to call the police. Ronnie sat in front of him laughing.

"You don't have a phone."

"Why are you here? Don't you think you have caused enough trouble?"

"Shh. Guys here's the news" Paul said.

Ronnie's father was still ranting and raving so Ronnie slapped him in the head.

"Shut it, or I'll give you something to shout about."

The boys looked on in shock, as they had never seen Ronnie act like that before. They all looked back at the screen while the reporter recited a complete fictional story of what happened.

"The gang of boys, who are suspected of torturing and killing their mentor Brian Malliff, were seen several days ago fleeing from a house where a security warden from their Unit was found strangled. The gang is believed to be led by teenager Michael McDonnell."

The screen focused away from the reporter to show a photo of Matty and all the boys laughed.

"What the hell have you boys done?"

Ronnie's mother shouted as she stood in the doorway holding two large plates of toast.

"Here, let me help you with those Mrs Martin" Robbo said taking the plates from her shaky hands.

Before Robbo got the chance to sit back down several hands appeared and the plates were soon emptied and the boy's attention was soon back to the TV screen.

"D.C.I. Smith of Tayside Police released a statement saying that these boys are violent and dangerous and should not be approached under any circumstances. If members of the public come across any of these boys, they should contact the police immediately."

Mikey changed the channel.

"Where do we go from here?" Paul asked.

"Ask our leader" Alonso said.

"Which one" Paul said.

He looked at Mikey then to Matty continuously. The rest of the boys laughed, except Matty who gave Mikey a snide look. As the boys discussed their options Ronnie's Uncle Jimmy appeared in the doorway.

"What the hell is going on here? Is that my beer?"

"No, that WAS your beer. Now it's ours" Ronnie said.

"Oh, so now you have your little gang with you, you think you're some sort of hard man."

"There's no 'sort of' about it" Mikey said.

Jimmy stepped forward to go for Ronnie but Mikey quickly stood up to block his path. Jimmy was a big man and towered over Mikey, he had rough features that made many men squirm when confronted by him but due to his chosen life of alcohol abuse, he was relatively thin due to Mikey's broad shoulders.

Jimmy laughed "And what do you think you're going to do?" he gritted his teeth and screwed his face up.

Jimmy's expression, along with his aggressive attitude had in the past, made many hard men back down from him but Mikey was unfazed. Ronnie had seen the expression many times and cringed at the thought of what would usually come with it. Robbo stood up and took a step towards Mikey. Matty looked at the others and they all stood up except Ronnie, who stayed seated. He smirked at Jimmy. Jimmy looked around the room at the young boys' faces and could tell that lurking behind those innocent staring eyes, was a violence and hatred that was waiting to erupt. Although Jimmy had always acted tough throughout his life, he knew his limits. Even through the effects of alcohol, he knew how far he could go before walking away. This is one of those times. He turned on his heels and walked out of the living room into the kitchen. He saw the bottle of vodka next to the sink and decided to pour himself a drink. Images of Ronnie as a little kid flashed through his mind and he put the cup aside and gulped the vodka straight from the bottle. He thought of all those times when he knew he should have stepped in, when his brother was beating his poor defenceless boy black and blue. Instead, when his brother got tired he would sometimes take over. He even found it funny when his brother had to use his belt to hit Ronnie as his punches did not have the same effect.

Ronnie walked through to the kitchen to see his uncle Jimmy crouched on the floor with the bottle in his hand. Jimmy rose to his feet and stood inches from his face. He wanted to ask him why he hated him so much. He actually had a list of questions he wanted to ask, but instead, Ronnie stood silent and stared at him. He could smell the rotten alcohol from his breath.

"What's the matter? Do you want to hit me? Go ahead."

All the memories of abuse by Jimmy came flooding back to him.

"Hit you. You deserve to be in a wheelchair next to that piece of shit next door."

Ronnie titled his head back brought it forward to meet the bridge of Jimmy's nose and he crumbled to the floor. He looked up to see Ronnie standing over him with the same look and gritted teeth that he had shown him when he was a little boy. Jimmy began to feel remorseful for what he did to Ronnie and tears started running down his cheek.

"Why are you crying? It's only wimps that cry. Do you remember you used to say that to me? Do you remember you used to tell my father to hit me harder if I cried? It will toughen him up you used to say. Well it toughened me up alright. Tough enough to take a beating from both of you and still walk away. The only reason you are not in a wheelchair like that pathetic excuse I have for a father is because you weren't there that day. The day I realised why I was taking those beatings. It was to stop my mother from taking them, the same mother who did nothing to stop me from getting those beatings in the first place. The same mother I caught in bed with you."

Jimmy looked up through his tears.

"Oh did I forget to mention that before. Look at you, you're pathetic. Sitting there feeling sorry for yourself."

Ronnie turned to walk away and saw all his friends standing in the doorway.

"How long have you guys been stand..."

"RONNIE" Mikey shouted.

Ronnie turned to see Jimmy with a bread knife in his hand. As he lunged forwards, Ronnie quickly put his hands up to protect himself and the knife sliced through Ronnie's arm. Jimmy came at him again but Ronnie managed to get out of the way of the knife. He moved in close to Jimmy to try and relieve him of the knife. They wrestled from one side of the kitchen to the other and Ronnie managed to turn Jimmy's wrist away from him so that the blade was facing outwards, Jimmy was shouting that he was going to kill him. Mikey stepped forward to try and help but the pair stumbled backwards and Jimmy tripped over Mikey's foot. Both Jimmy and Ronnie stumbled to the floor. Ronnie got up quickly and grabbed a towel to wrap around his arm. He looked over at the other boys who were staring down at the floor behind him. He looked around to see Jimmy's body lying motionless on his back with the knife sticking out of his stomach. They all stood in shock as Ronnie's Mother squeezed past and let out a scream.

"Get her out of here" Ronnie shouted.

Robbo put his arm around her shoulders and took her back to the living room.

"Is he dead?" Paul asked.

"Feel free to check" Mikey gestured to Paul with his hand.

"No, I think he's dead" He said, satisfied with his observation.

"What are we going to do now?" Alonso asked.

No-one answered.

Mikey marched past everyone and into the bedroom. He took the quilt off the bed and walked back into the kitchen and placed it over Jimmy's body.

Matty helped Ronnie clean up the blood from his arm. He ripped up a dish towel and wrapped it around tightly to stop the blood flow.

"You really need some stitches in that."

"Well I can't exactly turn up at the hospital can I?"

"Come on you guys let's go next door" Mikey ushered everyone into the living room.

Alonso walked in first and picked up a tin of beer and opened it.

"How does it taste now?" Robbo asked.

"Quite good actually"

Ronnie picked one up next.

"Well I guess he won't need them now."

"How dare you. You are evil. You have just killed him and now you think it's funny" Ronnie's mother said.

"I wasn't the one who picked up the knife, he was. He shouted that he was going to kill me, so I'm quite sure he had it coming."

Ronnie's Mother leaped from her seat and started laying into him with punches and kicks. He grabbed her and threw her across the room.

"It should have been you lying next door, not Jimmy" She shouted.

"Why, so that you can carry on sleeping with him"

Ronnie's father turned his head swiftly to look at his mother.

"Oh did you not know" Ronnie said with a smug grin on his face.

Ronnie's father turned his head and gave him a scowl. The rest of the boys sat in silence drinking their tins of beer. They stared at the television but occasionally glanced at each other as they tried to blank out the drama going on around them.

"I think it's maybe time for us to move on" Matty said.

"Where are we going to go? The police will be all over the place by now" Robbo said.

"Why don't you take your friends to your lying little girlfriend's house? Oh, but her father moved to keep you away from her. What is she going to think of you now that you're a murderer? All of you, bloody murderers" She shouted.

Ronnie caught Mikey's eye and nodded towards the door.

"Right guys, I think it's time to go" Mikey said.

All the boys stood up to leave, much to the annoyance of Matty.

"Where are we going?" Robbo asked.

Mikey shrugged "We'll work it out."

The rest of the boys followed Mikey to the door while Alonso picked up the rest of the tins of beer.

"I thought you said it was disgusting" Paul said.

Alonso smiled back through his now, slightly intoxicated vision.

On the way towards the front door the boys had to walk past the kitchen and each of them looked at the now blood soaked quilt covering Jimmy's body. Once outside the boys realised they were running out of places to go. It was still early morning and the streets were beginning to get busy with people travelling to work. Matty took charge and announced he was going to Harvey's flat.

"He's our last hope of getting help to prove that we didn't kill Brian."

The rest of the boys nodded in agreement, accept Mikey, who silently had other ideas about the situation.

Chapter 13

Councillor Williamson had been awake from the early hours planning his speech. An interview had been arranged by the local newspaper for mid-morning. He was optimistic that it would lead to one of the nationals getting in touch and possibly one of the TV stations. The more lies he could spread the harder it would be for any of the boys to defend themselves. The whole situation had gone way beyond anything he could have ever imagined. He stood in his best suit admiring himself in the mirror when his phone rang and interrupted his devious thoughts. It was Frank.

"Councillor, they're on the news again. The police discovered their hideout but they managed to escape."

The Councillor did not reply. He hung up the phone and went downstairs where his wife was cooking his breakfast. His usual greasy fry up did not appeal to him today as he wanted to get to his office as soon as possible.

On arrival at the office, Williamson saw Frank waiting outside with Harvey, his latest employee. The Councillor took several deep breaths as he approached them and barely noticed Rosie's absence as he walked past. The Councillor stepped into his office and Frank and Harvey followed. He took off his suit jacket to reveal his massive frame and turned to face them with his large fake grin. He tried to sound as genuine and concerned as possible for Harvey's sake. He thought of it as a dry run for the cameras later that morning. He offered the boy tea or coffee and placed a large plate of his tempting gold foiled wrapped biscuits in front of him. Frank's hand hovered over the plate before it was put down. Frank rarely witnessed this side of Williamson. He knew it was all a show for the boy's sake, but he also knew what was coming. Williamson was drawing him in before getting what he wanted and then he would find a way to get rid of him. Harvey wasn't stupid. He was intelligent enough to know when he was being played. Having encountered Frank's intimidation on The Program, he was immediately suspicious of the whole situation. Frank had shown his true colours while on The Program, he was a bully. And now, as he squirmed in his seat in front of Williamson, Harvey realised who Frank answered to. Once the small talk was out of the way, Williamson went to work on Harvey by asking him about the other boys. Where would they be most likely to hide out? Had he seen them or had they contacted him? Harvey's answers were not enough to convince Williamson that he was telling the truth and he began to get impatient. He slowly paced his office floor talking about The Program and how much he respected Brian and wanted to help the boys before they got into any more trouble. He walked behind the large comfortable chairs where Frank and Harvey were sitting and with one large swoop he threw his arm around Harvey and grabbed him by the throat. He picked him up out of the chair and dragged him backwards to pin him against the wall.

"Tell me where they are?" He shouted.

Harvey started to choke and tried his hardest to pull Williamson's hands away but he was too strong. Williamson gripped tighter and Harvey struggled to breath.

"Councillor" Frank shouted.

Williamson looked at Frank and back to Harvey who was seconds from passing out. He released his grip from Harvey's throat but used the other hand to grab his groin.

"Where are they?" He shouted.

"I don't know. I haven't seen them" Harvey coughed and spluttered.

Williamson let him go and casually walked back to his seat behind his desk. He gestured for both of them to sit down again. Williamson took out a thick envelope from his drawer. He smiled at Harvey and threw it on his desk.

"It's yours. Take it."

"What is it?"

"Call it a working bonus if you like. Take it" He gestured to him.

Harvey looked at Frank who nodded at him to take it. As he leaned forward and gripped the envelope, Williamson grabbed his wrist and leaped up out of his seat. His screwed up face was inches from Harvey's.

"Now you take that envelope and you make sure you treat yourself well with what's in it. And if these friends of yours come knocking on your door. You be sure to tell Frank here."

He let go of Harvey's wrist and his face dropped to show his fake smile once again.

"Now off you go and wait outside while I go over some things with Frank."

Harvey walked shakily out of the office. As soon as the door closed behind him, Williamson stared at Frank. He pointed his finger at him as if he was scolding a child.

"If you ever butt in again when I am questioning someone, it will be the biggest mistake you ever make. Now go and drive him home and make sure he understands the situation."

Frank walked out of the office and Williamson sat back in his chair with his smug grin.

"Stop the car" Harvey said to Frank.
"Why, what's wrong?"
"Just stop the car."

Harvey opened the door and vomited by the side of the road. He closed the door and looked at the envelope in his hand. He had been bought and Frank knew exactly how he felt. He was once in the same position many years ago.

"Don't worry it will pass."
"Excuse me."
"That guilty feeling, it will pass."

Harvey looked at him in disgust. They arrived at Harvey's block of flats and as he opened the car door Frank grabbed his arm.

"Look, you don't have to get involved. If your friends get in touch, all you have to do it let us know."

Harvey pulled his arm free and gave Frank a stare before he slammed the door shut. He ran up the stairs of his building but before he reached his door he stopped. He looked at the envelope and tore it open. His eyes widened. It was a bundle of fifty pound notes. He hurried to his door and fumbled around with his key due to his excitement. Once inside he went to the kitchen and started to count it. He found a place to hide it under his sink and sat down. Seconds later he pulled it back out and looked at it. He smiled from ear to ear then began counting it again.

***

It was the morning of Billy's departure back to Scotland and he was unsure of what lay ahead. He was about to travel by cargo ship back to Liverpool docks and from there he would travel by train to Edinburgh where a friend would pick him up and drive him the rest of the way to Dundee. He called Kevin again to make sure that his arrival would be away from preying eyes. Kevin reassured him that he would be safe and informed him of the news of another murder. There was no turning back now, Mikey needed his help. Before Billy boarded the ship, he said goodbye to a tearful Nina and promised her he would be back.

***

Councillor Williamson marched towards his office after his long lunch break. The receptionist walked by his side informing him of his messages. He stepped into his office and closed the door while she was in mid-sentence.

"Fat arrogant pig" she muttered to herself.

The Councillor sat down at his desk which was covered in small yellow post-it notes with names and numbers. He scanned through them quickly but none of them appeared to be important enough for him to call back straight away. He had been hoping for a call back from one of the national newspapers or television stations seeking an interview on the now triple murder spree.

"Councillor, Detective Chief Inspector Smith for you" The receptionist announced through the intercom.

"Tell him I'm busy. I'll call him back."

"No I mean he's here, he's outside your office."

The Councillor was slightly embarrassed in knowing that Smith would have heard this. He thought to himself that he would have her fired within the week. He opened his office door to find Smith accompanied by his partner Nevin. He introduced himself and reached out his hand to Smith, he smiled at Nevin but did not offer the same courtesy handshake as he did Smith.

"Come in, have a seat. Would you like some tea or coffee?"

"Coffee would be good thanks" Smith said and Nevin nodded with a thanks.

"Mary, could you bring in a tray of refreshments please."

One of the perks Smith liked about his job was that wherever he went he was always offered tea or coffee. After the introductions were out of the way, Mary appeared with a pot of coffee and the usual tray of luxury biscuits. Smith sometimes wondered why council officials and business men were mostly large fat people and after observing the treats in front of him, he thought that this was probably a main contribution.

Smith had known of the Councillor's reputation and how ruthless he could be in a board room. He had heard people say it was one of the main reasons he was elected, for his no-nonsense, straight to the point attitude. He was well respected in the business world for his honesty and people thought that if he was voted in, he would give the existing councillors a good shake up. The talk now is that he is still as ruthless as a councillor as he was as a businessman, but only when he was lining his own pockets.

Smith leaned forward in the large leather chair that was facing Williamson and looked around his office, he took in the fine décor and marble floors, the best that tax payers' money could buy.

"So how can I help you?" Williamson said in his best suave tone that he perfected for moments like this.

"Well we are currently working a murder investigation that is linked to a rehabilitation unit called The Program."

"Tragic, tragic, I heard there was another murder this morning I hope you catch those boys soon detective."

"Yes well, I heard you are a man who likes to get straight to the point so if you wouldn't mind answering a few questions to help with our enquiries."

"Sure, go ahead."

"You had three staff working in the unit from your department."

"Yes that's right. Frank, Bruce and Scott"

"Can you tell me why there were members of staff from your department employed in the unit?"

"It was all to do with funding. You see, The Program was only granted a certain budget per year. So where some departments have larger budgets, we move staff around to accommodate them."

Smith knew full well why they were on The Program, but proving it was another matter.

"I noticed that one of your receptionists, Rosie, is absent. We were hoping to have a chat with her."

Williamson had not been concerned about Rosie's absence, until now, but he was confused as to why they would be enquiring after her.

"Do you have an address for her?"

"I'm sure it will be on file, I'll have one of my other assistants look it up for you. Can I ask why you need to talk to her?"

"We just need her to help clear up a few of our enquiries."

Smith knew he had his attention. He had planned out his questioning to keep Williamson focused on him while his partner studied his reactions.

"Did you know that Rosie was Scott's sister?"

Williamson was lost for words. His mind was racing as to what to reply.

"Eh, no I never knew that."

"We've been trying to contact her since the night of her brother's murder but she appears to have vanished. We can't trace her or her car."

Williamson shrugged his shoulders.

"If I hear anything you'll be the first to know."

Smith looked down his page of notes again and skipped a few. He knew he had caught Williamson off guard with the sister thing, so he decided to go for it.

"Do you know anything about a complaints book?"

"Sorry, a what"

"You know a note book. It was kept by Brian Malliff in his office and it apparently contained a list of complaints."

"Complaints about what exactly"

"Your staff"

"I'm sorry, but this is news to me."

"Uh huh" Smith lifted his head from his notes to look Williamson straight in the eyes.

"Excuse me Detective, but I'm not sure where this is going. Are you accusing me of something?" Williamson's tone had changed dramatically.

"No, not at all, I'm simply asking if you have any knowledge of the whereabouts of the complaints book."

"Look, I don't know anything about any complaints book, and I certainly don't like any accusations to-wards my staff."

Williamson was rattled now and his voice was becoming louder and more aggressive.

Smith looked at Nevin and nodded.

"Well, I think that will be all for now."

They both stood up but Williamson stayed seated. His anxiety was making him sweat profusely. He leaned back in his chair and clasped his hands tightly while he watched the detectives leave. Smith reached the office door and turned back.

"Oh, eh, Thanks again for your time, and for the coffee" He smiled.

The office door closed and Williamson leaned for-ward in his chair, he picked up the receiver and dialled a number.

"Frank"

"Yeah"

"We need to talk. Come up to my office as soon as possible."

He hung up the receiver and leaned back in his chair once again while he considered his next move.

Chapter 14

After leaving Ronnie's parent's house the boys were running out of places to hide. Hunger was a major problem and this resulted in the boys arguing constantly. Matty had tried to show his authority over the other boys by urging them to go to Harvey's house, but to his disappointment, they all sided with Mikey and decided that it was a bad idea. Ronnie had not said a word since leaving his parent's house and each time one of the boys asked him if he was okay, he replied with a grunt.

They walked for several miles through back streets and waste ground to avoid being seen. Whenever they heard police sirens in the distance and the sound appeared to be coming closer to them, the boys froze, thinking they had been sighted. The weather had started to turn cold, so after coming across a derelict building, they made a quick decision to hide out there until dark. The building was adjacent to an industrial estate. Most of the windows were boarded up and where the boards had been removed, the windows were smashed. One of the window frames had been taken out and this was where the boys climbed through. It was previously a small factory and parts of old machinery had been strewn across the floor, anything of value was taken long ago. There were several doors located to the rear of the building and upon closer inspection; Robbo announced that one of them was a toilet after retching at the smell. Matty walked into a small room that was dimly lit from the small holes in the boards covering the windows. The floor was carpeted and in the middle of the room was a desk with some broken chairs scattered around. After walking all morning in the cold and rain the small office felt warm to the boys. Ronnie walked in and found a space on the floor and sat down. He chose the darkest corner and curled up with his back against the wall and his knees up close to his chest. The other boy's followed suit with hardly a word said between them as they closed their eyes. Some of the boys managed to fall asleep but it did not last as they would jerk themselves awake at the slightest noise. By late evening, the small light they had coming in through the gaps in the boards had disappeared. The six boys sat in silence in the darkness shivering and hungry.

"So what's our next move Matty?" Robbo asked.

"I think we should go to Harvey's."

"That's what they will expect us to do. They will have someone watching him and no doubt he will have been pulled in and warned anyway" Mikey said.

"Warned about what?"

"That if he helps us, he will be an accessory"

"Right now, I don't care. We can't keep going like this" Paul said.

"We could at least check it out. See if his place is being watched, if not, we could get some food and heat" Alonso said.

Although Matty was their official leader, Mikey knew that the comments were directed at him. He knew he had their backing and they would go with his decision.

"What do you say Mikey? Do you want to check it out?" Paul said.

"If you guys want to go, I'm in, but I really think this is a bad idea" Mikey conceded.

"Well if you have any other suggestions I'm all ears... Come on, you seem to always have all the answers." Matty snapped. He was showing his authority now that the boys had come around to his decision.

Mikey didn't take him on.

Matty stood up and worked his way along the wall until he reached the door. Outside of the room there was enough light coming through to find their way back out of the building.

The temperature outside had dropped and the boys felt the cold hit them straight away.

"Which way do we go then Matty?" Robbo asked

"I don't know I thought maybe one of you guys would know. Ronnie?"

Ronnie shrugged his shoulders "I know where Harvey lives but I don't know how to get there as I don't know where we are."

"Oh great, now we're lost. Whose stupid idea was it to come here anyway?" Robbo asked.

The rest of the boys looked at Matty.

"It wasn't me."

"You led us here Matty, you were the one out in front" Robbo said.

"Wait a minute. If Ronnie hadn't been so handy with that knife, we wouldn't have had to rush off in the first place" Matty blurted out.

The boys all looked around at Ronnie and half expected him to lunge at Matty but he shrugged his shoulders and wandered off.

"Good one Matty" Paul said.

"Ronnie hold up" Mikey walked fast to catch him up.

"I need food" Ronnie stated.

"Ronnie we know it wasn't your fault, Matty was just being a dick. We're all sorry about what happened with your uncle. "

"I don't care about him. I don't care about any of my family."

"Well what's wrong?"

"I need to find somebody."

"Who"

"A friend, I need to find her and let her know the truth."

"The girl you're mother mentioned."

"Lesley-Ann"

"Who is she?"

Ronnie looked back at the other boys who were trailing behind them and slowed his pace down a little. She's a friend who lived near me. She stuck by me the whole time I was in trouble. She knew everything that was going on and was a witness when my case came up. Not that it mattered because I was locked up anyway. Her father moved her away before I got a chance to thank her. He even made her change schools so I couldn't see her. When Brian took me on The Program I told him about it and he tried to help. He found out her new school and contacted her father but he told Brian that he didn't want me near her.

"At least you tried mate."

"It's not that, with everything that's happened and all that stuff in the papers she might start believing it."

"Come on Ronnie. If she knew what you went through and stuck by you all that time, she's not going to change her mind about you now."

"I know, but I would like the chance to talk to her. Even for a few minutes. You know, just to reassure her."

"Look Ronnie the rest of the guys seems to think this Harvey is going to help them, why don't we go along with it and see what happens. If nothing comes of it I'll go with you to the school and we'll find her for you."

Ronnie stopped walking and thought for a few seconds.

"Okay, but don't tell any of the others about this."

"Of course not" Mikey smiled.

The boys walked on until they reached the main road at the end of the industrial estate. Ronnie's depressed mood appeared to have lifted and he was now walking with a light spring in his step. Straight across from them was the start of a small housing scheme and situated at the end of a row of houses was a large convenience store. Ronnie looked around at the other boys. He nodded at Mikey and looked over at the store. Mikey smiled.

"Let's do it" Mikey said.

"Don't be stupid guys, the place is too busy. We'll get caught" Matty said, but Mikey and Ronnie were halfway across the busy road dodging traffic. The rest of the boys followed and Matty reluctantly ran to catch up with them.

As they approached the shop there were cars parked out in front with customers coming and going. Paul, with his mischievous mind, clocked one of the car engines was running and there was no driver. With the thought of food on their minds and the excitement of raiding another shop, the boys walked past the local newspaper advertising board without noticing the latest headline about them.

£10,000 REWARD FOR INFORMATION LEADING TO THE ARREST OF NOTORIOUS GANG SUSPECTED OF TRIPLE MURDER

This was Williamson's latest brainwave. He officially put up the ten thousand pounds reward on behalf of Brian and Scott's families for the safe capture of the boys. Unofficially, if the boys were found dead the reward would still be paid.

The boys entered the shop one at a time and separated up the aisles. At first they were almost unnoticed as the owner was busy serving a line of customers. The boys began filling their pockets with bars of chocolate and packets of crisps and biscuits. It was not until Robbo went back up to the front of the shop to pick up a basket that one of the customers recognised him. He was standing in the queue looking over the front page of the evening newspaper while waiting to be served. He caught sight of Robbo and then stared at the photo in the paper. He then looked around the shop at some of the other faces. Robbo began filling the basket with ready-made sandwiches from the open fridge while the customer was informing the others in the queue of who the boys were. The police had informed the public not to approach the boys but Williamson knew that a reward of ten thousand would be too much for some to resist. Robbo had filled the basket, the boys had filled their pockets and Ronnie had filled his mouth. They were ready to go, ready to make their escape. Mikey looked up at the checkout. The owner wasn't there. He looked over at the door. The owner had the keys in his hand ready to lock it. The other customers were standing near him ready for their share of the ten thousand. This was about to go bad, really bad, Mikey thought. He looked over at the other boys and nodded at the door. The boys gathered at the top of the aisle out of sight of the front door.

"Guys there are six of us. We can take them."

Mikey's intentions were to charge at them and smash through the large window to escape.

"Where's Paul?"

The rest of the boys looked at each other and shrugged their shoulders. They started looking down the aisles when they heard a loud crash from the side of the shop. They looked up to see the one of shop front windows caved in and the grille of a car sticking through it. Mikey smiled when he saw the pair of eyes struggling to see over the dashboard.

"It's Paul" Mikey shouted.

Paul had the seat squeezed up tight to the steering wheel so that he could reach the pedals. He pressed the clutch down and slammed the gears into reverse while the boys made a run towards him.

"Hurry" He shouted.

The boys' faces lit up as they scrambled into the car. The shop owner, along with the other customers, began to give chase.

"That's my car." One of them shouted as he ran to catch them. Paul reversed out onto the road and the shop owner stood in front of the car with his hands up to signal them to stop. Paul put the car into first gear and revved the engine to taunt the shop owner.

"What are you waiting for? Let's go" Robbo shouted.

Paul looked at Mikey who was in the front passenger seat.

"Go for it Paul, he'll move" Mikey said calmly.

Paul smiled and put his foot on the accelerator until it touched the floor. The wheels screeched as the car sped towards the shop owner. There was a split second stand off until the shop owner came to his senses and realised that the car was not going to stop for him. His eyes widened and his jaw dropped before he dived out of the way. Paul headed through the housing scheme until he reached another main road. He cut across it and continued until he found a secluded area. They were hidden from any traffic but had a view of the street at either side. Paul kept the engine running to keep warm while all the boys stuffed their faces.

"Robbo, close your mouth. You eat like a pig" Alonso said.

"No I don't."

"Yes you do" They all agreed.

"Paul, how did you know to go for the car?" Mikey asked.

"I clocked it sitting outside with the engine running and nobody was in it and when you guys entered the shop I noticed the newspaper board outside. It said ten thousand pounds reward for capture of the gang. When I entered I noticed one of the customers at the till clocking you so I knew something was going to happen."

"I didn't even know you could drive. I would love to know how to steal a car" Alonso said.

"How do you think he ended up on The Program?" Ronnie said.

"Really, is that right Paul?"

"Well, not at first because it wasn't really stealing, it was more like taking a car without permission as the keys were still in the ignition. That's what we did before we found out how to hot wire. We would just kick a ball around outside the shops and every once in a while someone would come along that was in a hurry and think nothing of going into the shop and leaving the engine running. Then a friend of a friend showed us how to hotwire and that's when the trouble started."

"Wait a minute, if that's true about the reward for our capture, then that means it's not only the police out looking for us. It's everyone" Matty stated.

"You're right. Anybody and everybody will want their hands on that money" Alonso said.

"So where do we go from here?" Robbo asked.

"Anywhere we want" Paul smiled.

"What about Harvey. I thought we were going to see if he could help us. We have transport now, we can at least check it out" Matty said.

"I guess there's no harm in checking it out" Ronnie said.

Mikey shrugged "Whatever we do, we have to get rid of this car or we'll be caught straight away."

"So how do we get there?" Alonso asked.

"We can get another one. You did mention that you wanted to learn how to hotwire."

Mikey looked at Paul who nodded in agreement.

"Hold on, I've just had a thought. We have been walking about and hiding in sheds while all this time you could have been chauffeuring us around. Why didn't you mention this before?" Robbo asked.

"Because Brian made me see the error of my ways"

"You mean, we are all on the run for murder, well triple murder, according to the papers and you are worried about being caught stealing a car."

The boys all laughed.

"I can't figure you out Paul. I can't tell if you are really stupid or if it's just an act to make people think you are stupid" Mikey said.

Chapter 15

Smith drove up the road towards the convenience store. He could see the large crowd before he arrived on the scene. Through the commotion he could see the flashes from the reporter's cameras. He wondered if the people involved called the newspapers first to negotiate a fee for their story before they actually called the police. Officers were in the process of setting up barriers around the shop and as Smith was let through, he was met by Nevin who briefed him on the situation.

"Williamson's reward has only been in the paper for a few hours and we already have would-be heroes risking their lives for a quid."

"I think it's a lot more than a few quid."

"These boys are now going to be hunted like outlaws."

"Somehow I think that's Williamson's intention."

"Have you heard about the conditions of the re-ward?" She asked.

"Dead or alive" They both raised their eyebrows.

Smith looked around the scene. He couldn't help but think about Billy. Word would surely have reached him by now. Williamson had basically put a bounty on his brother's head, so it was only a matter of time before he made an appearance.

"We're setting up road blocks at every exit out of the city in case they've swapped cars, well, now that we know they can drive" Nevin said.

"That's wasting our resources."

"What do you mean Inspector?"

"Those boys aren't going anywhere. If they can drive, they would have been gone long ago. You have to try and think like these boys. They're not stupid. They've grown up being chased by the police. That car will have been dumped by now so our best chance is to search the schemes and back streets. We can maybe work out where the boys are heading if we find the car. Get me the addresses of the other two security officers from the unit.

"You don't think they'll go after them do you?"

"What do they have to lose? Set up surveillance at their addresses and let me know about anything unusual".

***

The boys sat in silence as a patrol car drove past them and then did a u turn in the main road before driving past them again.

"I think we should swap cars now Paul" Mikey said.

"Yeah I think that would be a good idea."

The boys stepped out of the warm car into the cold night and crossed the road into a quiet street. Paul led the way as the boys followed him into someone's garden. On the way around the back Paul picked up a large stone and walked straight over to the garden shed and smashed the padlock.

"Paul, what are you doing?" Matty asked.

"I thought you guys needed a car?"

"We do."

"Well, we need some tools."

Matty didn't answer and left Paul to it as he searched around in the darkness. He came across a tool box and pulled it out of the shed so that he could see better in the moonlight. He picked up a screwdriver and carefully placed the toolbox back into the same place he found it. He closed the shed door and walked away with the rest of the boys following him. Before he reached the front garden he picked up another stone. Paul was still out in front as they walked towards a busier street up ahead.

"Paul there was plenty of cars in that quiet street, why didn't you go for one of those?" Robbo asked.

"Think about what you have just said."

"What do you mean?"

"A quiet street, smashing a window, does that not register?"

Before the boys reached the main road, Paul told them to wait by the adjacent path.

"Ronnie you come with me, keep a look out."

The two boys walked up the street while the others watched and waited. Ronnie walked up to the first car and looked over at Paul.

"No not that one. Cross the road, come on" Paul whispered.

Ronnie followed him and stopped at a newer car that had large shiny wheels with a few small dents here and there. Paul shook his head. Ronnie was puzzled.

Paul marched up the street with Ronnie close behind.

"Will you just hurry up and pick a car." Ronnie snapped.

Paul stopped suddenly and crossed over the road again, he saw what he was looking for.

"That one, that's the one we need."

"Paul can you please tell me what was wrong with all those other ones?" Ronnie turned to look back down the street.

"Well, the first one you mentioned was a wreck, which means the owner doesn't care much for it, it could possibly be a stop gap until he has enough cash to buy a newer one, therefore he will only top up the fuel if and when he needs to, which for us, it means we wouldn't get very far with it. The sporty one you pointed out with the shiny wheels and the stupid looking bumpers attracts too much attention, which we definitely do not need. Now this one…"

Paul shattered the small back window with the stone.

"….This one is not much to look at considering it is a fairly new one. It has a boring shape and is polished to a high standard. There are no fancy wheels or body kit to draw attention. Some might say it is an old Fuddy Duddy's car."

Paul felt along the window and unlocked the door. He slid into the driver's seat and smashed the steering column using the brick and screwdriver. He then jammed the screwdriver into the ignition and turned it like a key. The engine started. He reached over to the other side and unlocked the passenger door for Ronnie.

"Now if you think about it, this car is well maintained and if you care to look at this little dial here, it will signal a full tank of petrol. Which I suspect the owner keeps for emergencies. Emergencies like ours."

"You little smart ass" Ronnie mumbled.

Paul turned the car around and flashed the lights to signal for the others to come.

The rest of the boys ran towards the car and the four boys squeezed into the back. Paul was busy flicking through the owners cassette tapes.

"Paul what are you doing? Let's go" Ronnie shouted.

"Just a minute, the owner has to have something decent here."

Ronnie faced the others in the back. He put his hands up with his palms facing up to signal his confusion. Matty shrugged.

"Ah here we are. The Rolling Stones, I knew the owner had to have something good in his life."

He slammed the tape into the stereo.

"A good Stones tape will see you through bad times more than a flashy car ever will" Paul turned up the volume and drove off.

"Paul you're really weird, you know that?" Ronnie said.

Paul ignored the comment as he continued trying to see over the steering wheel.

"So where are we going then guys?" Paul asked.

"Harvey's, we're going to Harvey's" Matty said.

"They'll be sitting waiting on us." Mikey said.

"Look guys. I need to know which way to go."

"Just drive Paul. We will work it out as we go" Ronnie said.

Paul took a few turns to finds a main road.

"Follow the city centre signs. At least if we do decide to go to Harvey's I know the way from there."

"I think we just keep driving until we're in another town and no-one knows us." Paul said.

"Our faces are in every newspaper in the country" Alonso commented.

"Well we'll go to another country."

"That sounds good to me, as long as I get to drive."

Upon reaching the city centre all the boys were arguing about where to go. Except Paul, who chose a lane in the road and followed it. The rest of the boys didn't realise until it was too late. He turned up onto the Tay Road Bridge.

"Paul, where are you going?" Alonso asked.

Paul smiled and sped up.

"I think you guys had better duck down" Paul said.

He turned up the stereo and pushed the accelerator pedal to the floor.

The car raced towards the tollbooth.

"Paul, stop, no" Matty shouted as the boys quickly ducked their heads down.

The car smashed through the barrier and cracked the windscreen.

Paul turned the stereo down "I always wanted to do that."

The boys all laughed.

"Why did you need the music so loud to do it?" Mikey asked.

"Well guys, in years to come, whenever you hear that song, you are always going to remember this moment."

"So much for not attracting attention" Ronnie said.

"At least you have all stopped arguing about where we're going. And I never heard any of you complaining when I crashed through the shop window."

"So where are we going?"

"Yeah, Paul, where are we going?" Alonso asked.

"I don't know, I just thought that maybe we should get out of the city for a while so we don't have to keep watching our backs every second."

"And crashing through a barrier on the Tay Bridge is really the way to go about it" Ronnie commented.

"Do you actually know which direction to go when we get across here?" Matty asked.

"No. I've never been across here. Have any of the rest of you guys?"

They all shook their heads. Paul reached the end of the bridge and drove around the roundabout twice before making a decision to turn off at the next left. He followed the road until he came to a junction. The sign had an arrow pointing to the left for Newport and another pointing right for Tayport.

"Okay Paul. Which one are we following?" Matty asked.

Paul wasn't listening. He was busy taking in his surroundings to help make his decision. He turned left.

"I guess we are going to Newport."

"I guess we are" Paul said.

"We don't even know what is here."

"I do."

"I thought you said you hadn't been here before."

"I haven't."

"We'll how do you know what's here."

"I don't. I'm just following the lights."

"What lights?"

Paul didn't answer but drove at a snail's pace along the narrow road. Mikey looked across the river and realised what Paul was doing. He leaned over towards Paul and pointed to his right.

"Are those the lights you are following?"

"What lights? What are you guys talking about?" Matty asked.

"Take a look to your right guys" Mikey said.

"I see it" Ronnie said.

All the boys' heads turned and looked back over the river. Paul pulled up and parked the car at the side of the road and the boys stared in amazement at the sea of lights.

"What? Don't tell me you guys have never seen that before?" Robbo asked.

"Never" Ronnie answered.

Paul drove further along the road and turned up to the left. He parked the car in a dead end street with the smashed front facing a brick wall. The boys got out and walked back to the main road. Ronnie pointed to a path which took them to a grass area close to the river's edge. They stood watching the wave's crash against the rocks below. Ronnie sat down on the grass with his feet dangling over the edge and stared out at the city that was lit up in the night sky.

"I'll bet you can sit here for hours looking at that" Mikey said as he sat down next to him.

"It looks a lot different from up there" Ronnie pointed up to the Law.

"Many times I've sat up there and often wondered what it would look like from over here."

The rest of the boys also sat down and not a word was said as they watched the flashing blue lights with sirens blaring at the start of the bridge. Each one of them drifted away in their own deep thoughts, blocking out the harsh reality of their situation. They were now becoming accustomed to the noise as they sat for a short while in silence enjoying the view, which was accompanied with the fresh sea air.

Alonso broke the silence "I'm getting cold again guys."

"Me too" Robbo said.

"So, what's our next move?" Matty asked.

"We definitely need another car?" Paul said.

"No. I mean where are we going from here?"

"I vote for getting another car and driving as far away from here as we can" Paul said.

"And do what?" Mikey asked.

"I don't know I've never been anywhere else."

"Me neither" Ronnie said.

"What about you Robbo?"

"I went to a lot of places with my mum but I was too young to remember much about them or even where we went. My dad was always too busy working to even take me to the park never mind out of Dundee."

"Alonso?" Mikey said.

"I've been to Chile."

"Where exactly is Chile?" Paul asked.

"South America"

"Wow. Can we drive there?"

The other boys laughed.

"What about you Mikey, were have you been?"

"Nowhere, that's my point. Not one of us has ever really left Dundee. We don't know our way around any other city. There is a reward out for our capture which means we couldn't trust anyone. Each one of us has grown up in different areas of Dundee and we know the streets and the places to hide."

"So what do we do Mikey? I mean, we can't run and hide forever" Matty said.

"But we haven't done anything wrong. We have to find a way to prove that. I think we should go after Frank and Bruce."

"And do what?"

"We capture one of them and force them to tell the truth about killing Brian."

Ronnie nodded "I'm up for that."

"Do you know where they live?" Matty asked.

"No, but you know someone who could probably help us out there" Mikey said smugly.

"Harvey. So now you want to go there?" Matty said.

"No harm in checking it out."

"So we go to Harvey's, we find out where Frank and Bruce lives, we capture one of them and make them tell the police what really happened." Alonso said.

The boys sat for a while longer looking out to-wards the bridge at the disruption they had caused and neither of them noticed that Paul had sneaked off in the darkness until they heard a car sounding its horn at the top of the path.

"I'll bet that's Paul" Mikey smiled.

"I never even noticed that he was gone" Ronnie commented.

The boys reached the top of the path to see Paul's cheeky smile behind the steering wheel. After the boys piled in, Paul casually drove back over the bridge unnoticed by the uniformed police who were busy controlling traffic on the opposite side of the bridge.

"Okay, take a left off this road Paul" Ronnie said directing the way to Harvey's flat.

After a few wrong turns Ronnie eventually found the correct street.

"Are you sure you know where you're going Ronnie" Mikey asked.

"I only ever went to Harvey's once with Brian, but I'm sure this is the street"

Mikey instructed Paul to drive along Harvey's street twice. He told the others what to look for.

"Guys, across the road, there is an unmarked car with two men watching the front door to Harvey's block" Robbo said.

Paul drove further down the street and parked be-hind a large work van. From one end of the street the car was hidden from view.

"Okay Ronnie, you go and see if he is in" Mikey said.

"Matty, you go with him."

"Why?"

"What do you mean why? You argued hard enough for us to come here, he's your mate, so go with Ronnie and see what's what" Mikey demanded.

Matty didn't have an answer for Mikey. He had been put in his place and knew it was not a good time to argue back. Both boys stepped out of the car and crept around the end of the block of flats, they climbed over a wall and two wooden fences until they reached the rear of Harvey's block.

"Which floor is it?"

"I don't know. I waited in the minibus while Brian checked on Harvey."

"Great."

Matty checked the names on the doors as they both ran up the flights of stairs. They stopped on the third floor.

"G. Harvey. This is it" Matty caught his breath.

He flicked the letter box and seconds later, Harvey opened the door and stared at them.

"What are you guys doing here? Do you know how much trouble you're in?"

"Graham, we're stuck mate, we really need your help" Matty pleaded.

"I can't help you. You're wanted for triple murder."

"Come on Harvey. You know we didn't do that" Ronnie said.

"How am I supposed to help you?"

"Look, can we come in and talk. There are policemen watching from outside."

Harvey hesitated for a few seconds and opened the door wider to let them pass. Matty walked in but Ronnie turned to go back down the stairs.

"Where are you going?"

"I'll have to go tell the others."

"What they're all here? You can't all come up here."

Ronnie ignored him and took the stairs two at time. Harvey tried to shout after him but he didn't answer.

"What in the hell happened Matty?" Harvey asked.

Matty was about to answer but was distracted by Harvey's large T.V. and stereo.

"Wow you must have a really good job mate."

"Yeah, I have a good job. Now what happened with Brian?"

"What is your job?"

"I do odd jobs for the council."

"What kind of jobs?"

"Never mind my job Matty."

Matty looked straight at Harvey.

"They killed him Brian."

"Who"

"You know who, Frank and Bruce."

"Did you see them do it?"

"No, Mikey did."

"Who's Mikey?"

"The new guy who replaced you on The Program"

"Who killed the other two?"

"Ronnie's uncle was an accident. We don't know who killed Scott."

"But you were seen running from his house."

"He was dead when we got there Graham, I swear."

"We went there to get him to help us but he was lying face down on his bed. It looked like he had been strangled. His whole house had been trashed."

The rest of the boys walked into the flat and wasted no time in making themselves at home. Harvey was immediately irritated by his unwelcomed guests who had taken over his flat.

"You guys can't stay here. I'm being watched."

"Yeah, we know. We saw them out front. They were too busy chatting and drinking their coffee to notice anything" Robbo said.

"Look guys, how do you actually expect me to help you? Do you know there is a reward for your capture? It's ten thousand pounds."

"Yeah, we thought we would be worth more than that. But then again we do have a Paki with us which kind of does bring the price down a bit" Robbo said.

Alonso was about to go for Robbo but Harvey stepped in.

"No, you're not starting this in here. I'm warning you. I can't believe you two are still at it."

"Still at it, they're worse than ever" Matty said.

"Do you know that unofficially, the reward is going to be paid out if you are captured dead or alive?"

The room went silent and the boys all looked at each other.

"The reward was only issued this morning and already there is talk of people coming to Dundee from all over the country to try and track you down. I think you guys should go and hand yourselves in now before one, or even all of you, are killed."

Matty looked at Mikey who in-turn nodded towards Harvey and he caught the exchange.

"What's going on?" He asked.

"Harvey. We need a favour."

"What kind of favour?"

Matty paused and looked around at the other boys.

"We need you to get Frank and Bruce's addresses."

"What? You can't be serious."

"They killed Brian. They obviously killed Scott as well but..."

"So what are you guys going to do, go and kill them?"

"That's not a bad idea" Mikey said.

The rest of the boys smiled at Mikey but he kept a straight face.

"Harvey, we're being blamed for Brian's murder. We need to get them to confess" Matty said.

"So what are you going to do, knock on their doors and say, please sir, could you confess to those murders we are accused of?"

"Well, not exactly, more like force them" Mikey said.

Harvey stood shaking his head at them.

"And what do you think Brian would say to all this?"

None of the boys answered.

"You guys know it's his funeral tomorrow right."

"Are you going?" Paul asked. "Do you think we could go?" He looked at Mikey.

The other boys also looked at Mikey and Harvey picked up on this. He stared at Matty for an answer as to what was going on.

"It will be swarming with police and reporters. They would pick us out in seconds" Mikey said before winking at Ronnie.

Ronnie smiled to himself.

Before Harvey left The Program, he knew that Brian had chosen Matty to take over his role as leader, but being in their presence it appeared that Mikey was now making the decisions for them. The all seemed determined that they were going after Frank and Bruce so Harvey knew he was never going to persuade them hand themselves in. Williamson's face flashed through his mind and he didn't want to imagine what he would do to him if he was caught helping them.

"He's right. They'll be expecting you guys to turn up at the funeral. Why don't you stay here when I go and I'll try to get their addresses for you?" Harvey said unconvincingly.

"So you'll help us" Matty asked.

"I can't promise anything, but I'll see what I can do."

Chapter 16

John Robertson Senior had run a successful building firm in the city for many years. He had taken over the firm from his father and built it up in the hope of passing it on to his own son, also named John. In the late seventies, when his father was still running the firm, the work was drying up and the business was suffering. They could not afford to employ extra staff so John would work late with his father every night and most weekends. John's only contact with his son was at breakfast as he would arrive home long after Young John had gone to bed. While the relationship with his son was strained through his absence, his marriage also began to suffer. Due to some expensive contracts that his father managed to secure with the local council, the work picked up and this had given him more free time to spend with his family, but it was too late, his wife was already in the middle of a full blown affair. She broke the news that she was leaving him for another man, an Asian man and Young John took the news very badly. Not long after, John Senior's father took ill and was forced into early retirement, this left John to run the business on his own, which meant the relationship with his son drifted further apart. He was regularly being called away from work to visit the school, as Young John was now a stroppy teenager and was constantly finding himself in trouble. John Senior's way of dealing with his son was to buy him off. He had seen it work in his business every day. If his employees were not happy, he gave them a pay rise. If his customers were not happy, he reduced their bill. When his son was playing up, he gave him anything he asked for.

John Senior had struck up a friendship with Brian Malliff many years before when he received a request from him to help with a fundraiser that he was organising. Like most people who knew Brian, John Senior had a considerable amount of respect for the work he did by helping young teens that had lost their way. John Senior knew all about Brian's new Program and the constant rejections from Councillor Williamson. He himself had clashed with Williamson many times over the years and knew that the other board members, through fear, backed his decisions.

With the constant threat of his son being placed into an Institution, John Senior saw an opportunity to maybe help him and Brian. He put forward his proposal of funding The Program for three years and made it public, and this placed the board under enormous pressure to reverse their decision on appeal. Williamson stubbornly rejected The Project without any explanation but was outnumbered by the other board members who gave their approval.

In the first six months of the program John Senior had heard good reports from Brian about his son's progress although the racial hatred was still a problem. In the month previous to the boys finding themselves on the run, John Senior had a home visit from his son. It was the first time they had talked without arguing in a long time and John knew this was due to Brian's influence. He had overheard the comments about his troubled son, whether it was through work or down at his local pub and he knew people were pointing the finger and blaming him for the way Young John had turned out. He ignored most of them, simply because he knew they were right. But if there was one thing he did know about his son, it was that he was definitely no murderer. He knew the respect his son and the rest of the boys had for Brian, so for any of them to turn on him, simply did not make sense.

On his way home from work, John stopped off at his local newsagents for cigarettes. He impulsively picked up a copy of the evening paper. He knew it would be filled with overblown lies about his son. Over the last few days, he had been disgusted when he read the stories about all the boys, building up each one of them to be guilty before any of them had a chance to defend themselves.

He arrived home and threw the newspaper on the dining table and went to the kitchen to prepare his dinner. On his return, he placed his plate down and slid the paper towards him. He was about to take a bite of his dinner when he read the headline confirming a reward for the gang. The story was accompanied with a photo of Councillor Williamson and continued onto the next page where it contained another photo of Williamson holding a cheque. John shook his head and carried on eating his dinner but was soon interrupted by the phone. He quickly marched over to answer it in the hope that it was good news about his son.

"I take it you know about the reward." A friendly voice asked.

"Yeah, I'm actually just reading it now. Is there anything that guy won't do to get himself in the papers?"

"You seem very calm about it."

"Well, if it gets my boy home quicker."

"John, I've heard from a good source that Williamson is going to pay out that reward, dead or alive."

"Can he really do that?"

"He's denying it."

"Putting up that reward is basically saying that my son is guilty."

"These boys are now going to be hunted like animals."

The line went silent. John felt nauseous.

"John, are still there?"

"Yeah, I'm still here" He answered in a croaky voice. "I'm going to see Williamson in the morning."

"It's Brian's funeral tomorrow."

"Great. Williamson has timed this perfectly hasn't he? The full line-up of press will be out and he will be doing interviews about this bloody reward."

John hung up the phone and looked over at his dinner. His appetite had gone. He took the plate and scraped the food into the bin. He went into the living room and flicked the channels on the T.V. in the hope of catching the news but it was not scheduled for hours yet.

He picked up the paper again. There was a police hotline at the foot of the page for the public to call if they had any information about the boys. Still clutching the paper, he picked up the phone and made the call.

"This is John Robertson Senior. I would like to talk to whoever is charge please."

The call was placed on hold for several minutes and was eventually answered by Smith "Hello John, this is D.C.I. Smith, how can I help you?"

"You can help me by telling me what the hell is going on."

"I assume this is about the reward."

"Of course this about the reward, my son is about to be hunted like a bloody outlaw."

"Look I know this is a stressful time but I can reassure you we are doing all we can to make sure those boys are returned to safety."

"Safety, Williamson is about to pay out that reward if those boys are found dead or alive."

"Can I ask where you received this information?"

"It doesn't matter where. I want to know what you are doing about it."

"Mr. Robertson, I can assure you that if we had evidence that someone was going to pay an individual to take the law into their own hands we would arrest them. We have received the same information as you and we are working on it. We need to trace the source of this information. We will also be questioning Councillor Williamson as to his knowledge of this information."

"So by the time you get around to questioning him, some idiot will have taken my son's life in the knowledge that they will be £10,000 better off" John slammed the phone down.

He went to the fridge and opened a bottle of beer. Twenty minutes later, he opened another. Over the next few hours he sat in deep thought about his son as he drank beer after beer until he passed out on the couch. He woke early in the morning in an uncomfortable position with the T.V. still on. A little unsteady, he made his way to the kitchen and put the kettle on. He had to pull himself together as he was about to pay Williamson a visit. After some strong coffee and a shower, he drove to the council offices. It was early and Williamson would not be there yet. If he had called to make an appointment he would never see him. He knew Williamson could give people the run around for days, weeks if need be. He parked his car and made his way to the large entrance. The security and receptionist had been well briefed. They took his name and gave him an appointment time for later that day, an appointment that would never be kept. There would be a list of excuses as to why Williamson was not there. He waited outside. Ten minutes went by and it started to get busy. A large group of office workers were making their way into the building and John walked with them. The security guard gave them a quick glance and upon noticing they were workers he turned back to his newspaper. As the group walked towards the lift, John made a sharp exit to the stairs. He reached the top level and peered through a gap in the door. There was another security guard outside Williamson's door. His plan was to sneak into Williamson's office and wait on his arrival but with the security guard outside his door, he knew Williamson was already inside. John watched and waited. Williamson eventually appeared from his office and walked over to talk to one of the women at their desk. John had forgotten about Williamson's intimidating appearance and for a slit second, he questioned his actions. He thought about his son and was soon marching through the door.

"Williamson I want to talk to you" He said in a raised voice. John felt every pair of eyes on him and clocked the security guard storming towards him. He grabbed John by the arm.

"Take your hands away from me right now" He demanded.

The security guard looked at Williamson who waved him away. The last thing Williamson needed was John being manhandled out of the building and making a scene with the amount of reporters hanging around outside. The security guard backed off and John continued walking towards Williamson.

"Come on, we can talk in my office" He put on his fake smile.

He held the door open for John and instructed one of his assistants to hold all his calls. The door closed behind them and John stood rooted to the spot in front of Williamson.

"What the hell are you playing at?" He shouted.

"John, calm down. Take a seat and I'll explain."

Williamson walked behind his desk and sat in his own chair. It was positioned to keep him upright but his weight made him sink back allowing his gut to hang out. John was still standing. He was in a rage.

"John, please." He gestured to the seat opposite and John reluctantly sat down.

The chair was so comfortable he immediately felt at ease as his back sank into the chair. This was not going to plan.

"So what's this all about?"

"What do you mean? You practically put a bounty on my son's head."

"Hardly, I put up a reward for the boys' own good. We can't have teenage boys running around the city killing innocent people."

"Dead or alive, you're going to pay up."

Williamson laughed and shook his head.

"John, come on, do you honestly believe that if someone hurt any of those boys I am going to pay them ten grand?"

"Oh I know you won't pay it. But I know you released that information so that other people will believe it."

"John, John" He shook his head. "You of all people should know that you don't believe everything you hear."

John stood up.

"I'll tell you what Barnaby. If anything happens to my son, I'll be coming for you. I will dig up every dodgy deal that you think you have covered up and I'll destroy you."

Williamson stayed calm.

"Is that right? Well, you just remember and include your own building firm on that list?"

"My firm is clean."

Williamson forced out a laugh. "How do you think you're father gained all those contracts?"

"My father built that business through hard work."

Williamson smiled "I think it's time for you to leave."

John's throat was dry. His meeting with Williamson had not gone to plan. He turned around and walked out of the office. The security guard stood firm in front him with his arms folded. John barged past him and marched out of the building and headed straight for his car.

He took in a few long deep breaths before knocking on his parents' door. His mother answered.

"John, what's wrong? Is there any news on Young John?"

"No not yet. I'm here to see Dad"

"He's watching T.V. Have you eaten, would you like some breakfast?"

"Yeah, that would be good, thanks."

John wasn't hungry but he wanted his mother out of the way while he talked to his father.

"Dad"

"John. What's happened? Is it Young John?"

"I need to talk to you Dad."

John's father put the volume down on the T.V. and turned to face him."

"It's about the business. I need a straight answer."

"Sure son, what is it?"

"The contracts, the ones you picked up when the business was struggling, were they legitimate?"

"What do you mean?"

"Don't mess me around Dad. You know exactly what I'm asking. I've just left Williamson's office."

He looked his father straight in the eyes and he could tell what was coming. His father shook his head. John looked at him distraught.

"I think you need to go and see a solicitor because it's all away to come out."

"But how, why"

"Because he has just put a price on my son's head" John stands up to leave.

"Where are you going?"

"To dig up all the contracts made since I took over the business, because I'm certainly not going down for it."

Chapter 17

Billy stepped off the large cargo ship when it arrived at Liverpool docks. He had arranged it with a friend and paid cash, no questions asked. Security was minimal and the authorities were more concerned with inspecting the shipment than the crew on board. Billy hated sailing and had thrown up several times during the journey. He found this very ironic considering he worked with boats. The same ship would have two more long journeys before it would arrive back in the same dock. It had been discussed between Billy and the crew that there was a possibility of an extra person joining him on the re-turn journey. With the mention of more money, a nod of the head accompanied with a large smile was enough to convince Billy the deal was done. He left the docks and walked to the nearest taxi rank. He instructed the driver to take him to the train sta-tion. The next train to Edinburgh was not leaving for another hour yet. He phoned Kevin to let him know of his expected arrival time in Edinburgh and asked him to make arrangements for him to be picked up and driven the rest of the way to Dundee. He would have travelled on the connecting train to Dundee but Kevin had the station checked out. Smith had several police officers manning the exit. The photos of him in the paper were from the last time he was in police custody which was over ten years ago and although he looked different, there was still a possibility that a sharp eyed officer would pick him out. Billy decided not to take the risk.

With his cap pulled down over his forehead, he went to the newsagents and picked up two newspapers, he paid for them and walked through to the bar. After he ordered himself a drink, he took a seat away from the bar. He sipped his drink and picked up one of the newspapers. The front page was a large photo of a smashed shop front and a headline relating to the 'Gang' as they were now known. He quickly scanned through the story before turning a few pages to a photo of the shop owner, accompanied with his exaggerated version of events and how he risked his life to capture the violent gang. There is another photo of the getaway car which was found hours later and only two miles from the shop. The photo showed the car doors left open with the keys still in the ignition. There were biscuit wrappers and empty crisp packets strewn over the seats and floor. Billy smiled as he thought about boys parked up and having a picnic in the car by the side of the road, while the police were rushing around not too far from them in a major search operation. His smile disappeared when he turned to the next page and read a statement from Smith instructing people not to risk their lives for the reward being offered by Councillor William-son. Billy then started to think about the would-be heroes out to catch them. He knew he had to find Mikey soon. He looked at his watch and finished his drink before walking off towards the platform.

***

In the comfort of Harvey's flat, the boys found that they could relax for the night. They cleaned themselves up before having some proper food fol-lowed by a good night's sleep. By morning they were up early and had gathered around the T.V. to watch the latest news about them. The video footage of the stolen car being driven through the barrier was shown in slow motion.

"Look you can just about see Paul's head" Alonso said.

"Hey Paul, were you actually ducking or is that you sitting upright?" Robbo asked.

The boys all laughed and even Harvey, who had been mentally preparing himself to face Williamson, managed a smile.

After dodging more questions about his job, Harvey left the boys in his flat and walked to the nearest taxi rank. He had hardly slept as he tossed and turned at the dilemma of betraying his friends or crossing Williamson. His chest was tight and his stomach was in knots. He leaned over a wall and retched but nothing came up. He lit up another cigarette, his third since he got out of bed. Brian had convinced him to stop while he was on The Program but due to the stress of recent events, he had started again. The temptation to go back to harder substances was also at the back of his mind but at the moment, he had resisted. He was on his way to pay his respects to someone who would be so ashamed of him right now. Brian had done so much for him and he had let him down by accepting money from Williamson.

"Right guys let's go" Mikey said as he looked out of the window to see Harvey halfway down the street and the unmarked car following him.

"Where are we going, I thought we were going to stay here until Harvey came back?" Matty asked.

"We are going to pay our respects."

"We can't go there, you said it yourself that the place will be swarming with police."

"Don't worry about it, we will keep our distance."

Mikey looked at Paul and nodded.

"You ready?"

Paul took the car keys out of his pocket and jingled them.

Due to the large turnout for Brian's funeral, the police were in attendance on McAlpine Road outside the crematorium. This was mainly to direct the volume of traffic from blocking the road. When the hearse appeared at the gated entrance, the cameras of the small group of reporters clicked away. Williamson stood proud at the front of the large waiting crowd, and without the slightest hint of guilt, Frank and Bruce stood in their security uniforms close behind him. A procession of cars followed the hearse and one of them was the Lord Provost. Williamson, not one to miss a photo opportunity, had tipped off the press of his attendance and made his way over to greet the Lord Provost as he exited his limousine. Brian's family walked behind his coffin into the crematorium and the large crowd followed on. As the last of them disappeared through the large wooden doors, the police and reporters moved to the exit at the side of the building. All the while, six pairs of eyes watched silently through the thick bushes beyond the surrounding trees. Forty five minutes passed before the exit doors opened.

"Right guys you go back to the car and wait on me and I'll wait and see which car we have to follow" Mikey said.

"I'll stay with you" Ronnie said.

"Oh and Paul, keep the engine running we may have to move fast."

Mikey and Ronnie looked on as the crowd exited the building. Brian's family stood by the doors as friends hugged and shook their hands and said their condolences.

"There's Harvey" Ronnie said.

"I can see him, but who is he talking to?" Mikey asked.

They both moved towards the edge of the bushes for a better view. The crowd broke up a little and Frank came into view. They talked for a few minutes as Harvey looked around nervously. Frank gestured to someone else in the crowd and a large stocky man in a suit came over. Harvey looked scared and appeared to be pleading with them. The large man placed his arm around Harvey and patted him on the back. Bruce joined them and they all smiled at each other before the large man walked away.

"What's going on Mikey?"

"I don't know" Mikey shrugged.

Frank wrote something on a card and handed it to Harvey before he walked off.

"Somehow I don't think it will be safe for us to go back to Harvey's" Ronnie commented.

"I wasn't planning on it."

Frank and Bruce headed towards the car park and Mikey watched closely to see what car they got into.

"Right let's go" Mikey said, and they both scrambled back under the bushes through the gap in the wire fence they made earlier. Paul had the engine running ready to go.

Mikey sat up front to give Paul instructions. From the rear of the crematorium, Paul sped through the Ardler housing estate and come out close to the Admiral pub. He parked up close to the main road where they had a full view of the car park exit. The boys all sat in silence as they waited on Frank's car.

"That's it there" Mikey said.

Paul got ready to follow.

"No, wait. Keep your distance. If he looks in his mirror he will see us straight away."

Paul let a few cars go by before he pulled out. The long queue of traffic moved very slowly and the boys began to panic when they spotted a policeman up ahead. He was holding back the traffic to allow more cars to exit the car park. As they approached, the policeman looked straight ahead and Paul prepared himself to do a u turn across the middle of the road if necessary. The policeman waved them through and the boys all laughed as he was too busy concentrating on what was going on around him to notice them drive passed.

Frank drove into the Dryburgh area of the city and the boys were not far behind. Frank pulled into the side of the road and Paul did the same. Bruce got out of the car and after a few words were said between them, Frank drove away. Paul moved out slowly and watched Bruce enter his house.

"Paul speed up, we need to catch Frank."

Paul drove onto the dual carriageway and struggled to keep up. They came to a roundabout and as they lost sight of his car, an argument started about which direction to go.

"Over there. Quick" Alonso shouted, while pointing to a road on the right

In the distance they could see the tail of his car go up a small hill and turn left. Paul put the foot down and the wheels screeched as he turned sharp around the corner.

"Guys there he is. Duck" Mikey turned his back to-wards the window to hide his and Paul's faces as Frank stood locking his car door.

"Do you think he saw us?" Alonso asked.

Mikey looked back to see Frank walking casually to-wards his house "I don't think so. If he saw us he would be back in his car following us."

"So what's next? Where do we go from here?" Paul asked.

"We go back and wait on Harvey" Mikey smiled.

"Are you sure Mikey? I mean after what we saw earlier. Do you really think that would be a good idea?" Ronnie said.

Why? What did you see?" Robbo asked.

Ronnie was about to speak but Mikey turned and gave him a look.

"Uh eh, nothing, it doesn't matter" Ronnie mumbled.

Paul drove back to Harvey's street and the unmarked police car had not returned. They parked on the corner of an adjoining street. They were out of sight but still had a clear view of Harvey's block of flats. They didn't have to wait long on Harvey's return after they spotted him walking along his street looking like he had the weight of the world on his shoulders. Robbo opened the car door.

"Where are you going? Get back in" Mikey demanded.

"Why? He's home. Let's go."

"We're not going in. Watch, he'll be back out in a few minutes."

Ronnie nodded at Robbo to confirm what Mikey had said.

"Look, I'm squeezed up in the back here, can I at least get out and stretch my legs."

"Okay but be quick" Mikey said.

"Yes sir" Robbo said.

Minutes later, Harvey appeared back out of his block and was walking fast up his street.

"Robbo get in quick. Paul, start the car" Mikey shouted.

Harvey broke into a light jog, he had to get to a phone box fast and explain to Frank that the boys had gone.

"Hey, Harvey, where are you off to in such a hurry?" Mikey said as Paul drove up beside him.

"Oh eh, I was off to see a mate."

"Squeeze in. We'll give you a lift."

"I won't fit in there. There's not enough room."

"Robbo can climb into the boot."

"Why do I have to do it? Alonso is smaller than me, he can do it. He's used to travelling that way anyway" Robbo laughed to himself.

Alonso didn't find it funny. He lunged sideways and connected a punch to Robbo's head. Robbo jumped out of the car and started taunting Alonso to a fight.

"Robbo are you stupid, get in the car now, the police will be here any minute and you're causing a scene in the middle of the street" Ronnie said.

Matty got out and opened the boot for Robbo and he reluctantly climbed in.

"So where did you guys go?"

"We went to pay our respects to Brian" Ronnie answered sternly.

"What, you guys went to the funeral?"

"Sort of, so where was it you were rushing off to then?" Mikey asked.

"Well when I realised you guys had left, I thought I would head off to a mates house. Where are you guys going?" Harvey asked.

Nobody answered and Harvey started to get a little paranoid.

"What's going on, what are you guys up to? ...Matty"

Matty looked at him and shrugged.

"We told you last night, we're going to force Frank and Bruce to tell the truth about killing Brian" Mikey said.

"But I thought you needed his address."

"We do, did you get it?"

"Yeah I got it."

"We got it as well" Alonso blurted out.

Mikey turned quickly and stared at Alonso but he didn't know what was going on.

"What, what did I say?" Alonso was confused.

"How did you get it?" Harvey asked.

"We followed him from the funeral."

"Can we see the address you got?" Mikey asked.

Harvey handed it over and Mikey looked at it and smiled then handed it over to Ronnie.

"That's not Frank or Bruce's addresses."

"What do you mean?"

"We followed them and that's neither of their ad-dresses."

"Let me see" Matty said.

He read it and looked at Harvey.

"Who gave this to you?"

"I eh, I work with the council now remember, it was easy" He said unconvincingly.

Mikey looked at Matty with a smug grin but Matty never saw Harvey speaking to Frank and Bruce so he didn't know what was going on.

"When you followed them, are you sure it was their own house they went to?" Harvey asked.

"He's right you know. That could have been anybody's house they were at" Matty said.

Matty flicked the piece of card with the addresses on them into the front of the car.

"Are you guys going there now?" Harvey asked.

They all waited on Mikey to answer but Ronnie beat him to it.

"I'm hungry guys. Can we go and get some food first?"

"Ronnie you're always bloody hungry, I'd love to know where you put it all" Alonso said.

"So what's the plan, are we raiding another shop?" Paul turned to face Mikey.

"No need, we have Harvey with us now" Mikey winked.

Chapter 18

Smith sat back in his chair and looked at the large board in front of him containing photos of the six boys. Underneath each one was information about their background and previous crimes. On the wall to the right of the board was a map of Dundee with small coloured pins to indicate each incident or citing of their movements.

Nevin entered his office "There's a call for you on line two."

"Who is it?"

"They wouldn't say."

Smith picked up the receiver and Nevin left.

"Hello this is Detective Chief Inspector Smith speaking how can I help you?"

"Billy McDonnell was picked up at Edinburgh train station today."

"How do you….?"

The line went dead. Smith, although annoyed at being hung up on, smiled to himself at the information he had received. He knew whose voice it was and the information would definitely cost him dearly. He sat back in his chair still smiling while thinking that it was now time to personally step up the search. If he could secretly keep track of the boys' whereabouts it would only be a matter of time before Billy made his appearance. Williamson's £10,000 reward did have him worried though, as every 'would be' hero was now on the lookout to get paid.

Smith got out of his seat and stood staring at the map in front of him for a long time. He tried to place himself in their situation. He had been ridiculed by his staff for his decision to put a stop on the road blocks on the exits out of the city, when only an hour later they crashed through the barrier on the bridge. This could not have worked out better if he tried as those boys would have been in custody right this minute and his only chance of luring Billy back here would have been blown. Nevin had suggested to Smith the possibility of the boys making some sort of appearance at the funeral, so tactfully, he made sure extra officers were on duty in the hope of scaring the boys away from the scene.

"Word has come in from the two officers watching Graham Harvey's place" Nevin said as she entered his office.

Smith was about to make a comment about her lack of knocking, but he let it go and gestured for her to continue.

"He turned up at his flat after the funeral, left after a couple of minutes and got into a car at the end of his street, apparently the car was full and it looked like a young boy was in the driver's seat."

"Did they follow it?"

"No, they had specific instructions not to move but report anything unusual."

"And common sense didn't register that it could have been the boys? Did they get the registration by any chance?"

"They're running it through right now."

Smith turned and looked back at the map. He now started to think that if those boys were still mobile, then this opened a whole new list of possibilities of where they could turn up, and at the back of his mind, it gave him a much less chance of capturing Billy.

***

Billy was driven through his old haunts and hardly recognised them. He had been away for so long and travelled to so many different countries that he had forgotten what most of it looked like. The driver, a trusted friend of Kevin's, pointed out some of the old places that had been demolished to make way for new build homes and supermarkets. The driver took him to The Pheasant, a rough old pub on the outskirts of the city that Kevin had taken over several years ago. He drove him around the back, out of sight of any passers-by. The driver gave a light coded knock on the door and Billy was welcomed in with hugs and handshakes from Kevin and a few old friends. The driver had informed Billy before entering the pub that Kevin was already onto one of their 'friends' for divulging information to Smith. After the pleasantries are out of the way Billy wasted no time in getting down to business. As they sat around the small table in the back of the pub, Billy was brought up-to-date with the latest developments and was told a few truths that the newspapers would not dare print. Kevin was already on the trail of Williamson but he deliberately held back a few of the specifics of their plans and added in some false details for the grass to report back to Smith. After the driver was verbally given a fictitious address for Billy to hideout, Kevin secretly slipped him a piece of paper containing the correct hideout, unaware of the preying eyes in their company.

***

Paul drove onto the main road opposite a takeaway shop and was unaware of the unmarked police car that had picked up their trail only minutes before. As they sat in the car reciting their food order to Harvey, Mikey pulled out a small role of cash to pay for the food.

"Where did you get the money from Mikey?" Matty asked.

Mikey ignored him and the rest of the boys looked on with a smile as unbeknown to Harvey, they had found his hidden stash earlier that morning.

Harvey left the car and walked into the takeaway shop, he immediately clocked the payphone on the wall. He made the order at the till and paid the cashier and checked the change before putting it into his pocket. From where he stood, he had a clear view of the car across the street where the boys were waiting. He eyed up the payphone and then stared back over at the car. He sauntered over to the other side of the shop where a large pillar blocked his view. He was close to the payphone and when he looked out the window, he couldn't see the car. 'If he couldn't see them, then they couldn't see him' he thought. He took some of the change out of his pocket and lifted the receiver. He felt his heart beating faster as he dialled the number. Without even saying his name he passed on the information and walked back to the counter again. He glanced out of the window at the boys in the car. When his order was ready he left the shop.

"Did you get everything?"

Harvey's body shuddered with fright as he turned to see Mikey behind him.

"Oh eh yeah, I got everything. Where have you been?"

"I had to pee" Mikey said with a smug look on his face.

They walked back to the car where Harvey watched the boys eat like they hadn't eaten in days. Mikey gave Ronnie a sly wink to confirm what he had seen.

***

Smith had radio contact with his two officers, who were only metres away watching every move the boys made. He gave them specific instructions to keep their distance and not do anything to jeopardise their position. Smith put out a call for all patrols to be on standby and was about to rush out of the station when he received an urgent call. It was his informant with the address of Billy's hideout. Smith suddenly slowed down as he contemplated the situation. He wanted to capture Billy but he couldn't take the risk of sabotaging the tail on the boys.

***

During the journey to Bruce's house, Mikey no-ticed the same car passed them twice. The driver and passenger looked straight ahead so as not to arouse suspicion, which for Mikey, it did exactly that. Mikey instructed Paul to pull into the side of the road. They waited patiently to allow several cars to pass them. The officers tailing them radioed Smith in a panic, thinking they had lost them. Smith looked at his map and thought about the direction the boys were travelling and reassured his officers of where the boys were going. He called for all the units to cover every exit within a half a mile radius of Bruce's address.

***

Two men had sat for several hours in their beat up car listening intently to their police scanner.

"We've got them now, that ten grand will soon be ours" The driver said before he started the engine.

He sped off in the hope of beating the police to one of the exit points before they had the chance to set up their road block. The passenger was holding two weapons, tightly on his lap. One was a sawn off shotgun, the other was an old army pistol, both of the weapons had been dug up the same day that the reward for the boys was announced, and both had also been used by the two men in a failed robbery only months before. The same men were about to use them to capture the boys and claim the reward money.

***

The boys parked a few hundred yards from Bruce's house and Mikey could sense that something was not right. It was early evening, they were parked on a busy road and not a single car had gone by them. He also noticed that Harvey was acting a little strange and wondered if it had something to do with the phone call he made from the take-away shop. The boys stepped out of the car and as Mikey opened the boot to allow Robbo to climb out he made eye contact with Ronnie, who in turn nodded towards Harvey. Mikey instructed Paul to stay with the car and leave the engine running.

Unbeknown to the boys, as they made their way towards the rear of Bruce's house, they were being watched, but not only by police officers and armed vigilantes but also by the occupants of Bruce's house who had now gathered together after Harvey's phone call, and were now ready and waiting. Mikey quietly counted down the number of houses and intentionally pointed out the wrong one. As the boys gathered at the back gate to what they thought was Bruce's garden, Mikey informed them of his plan.

"Ronnie and I will go in through this gate to Bruce's back door. Matty and Harvey, you guys go in through the neighbour's and wait there. Robbo and Alonso, you guys do the same on the opposite side."

"Why?" Matty felt confused but relieved at the same time that he was not going in after Bruce.

"Because, if he manages to escape and does a runner there will be someone at either side to catch him" Mikey replied.

"What do we do when we catch him?" Harvey asked.

"The same as he did to Brian" Robbo mumbled.

"Robbo" Mikey nudged him to be quiet.

"I thought you said we were only capturing him and forcing him to tell the truth" Harvey said.

"We are."

Matty and Harvey made their way over to the neighbour's fence and watched as Mikey and Ronnie entered through the back gate. They did the same and were too busy watching next door to notice two dark figures creeping up behind them. The dark figures made their move and pounced on Matty and Harvey. As the two boys struggled and shouted out for help, Robbo and Alonso began to climb the fence to go and help them but were held back by Ronnie.

"Don't be stupid, it's a set up" Mikey whispered.

The boys crouched down in the darkness and watched as Bruce come charging out of his house followed by Frank and several others, all were armed with batons and torches. A shot was fired by one of the men and as Bruce hit the deck his torch rolled along the ground. The rest of the men backed off and ran for cover. Matty managed to free himself and also made a run for it. Another shot was fired and the boys watched through the darkness as the shadow of their friend fell to the ground. The loud shots from the pistol alerted the police who quickly swooped into action. One of the policemen first on the scene shone his torch on Matty's still, blood soaked body. He worked his way up with the torch to see one of the armed men with his arm around Harvey's neck and a sawn off shotgun pointed under his chin. As the police were unarmed, a call was made to headquarters to release the armed response unit immediately. Within minutes the whole neighbourhood was in chaos as people come to investigate the commotion. The officer that was on the scene tried to calm the situation by instructing everyone to keep their distance. The two armed suspects were surrounded by police and Smith attempted to talk to them in an effort to stall them until the armed response unit arrived. Mikey used the disruption to make his getaway. He tugged on the other boys' arms and led the way back out to the street. They blended in with the crowds that had gathered and enjoyed listening and adding to the comments being made about them as they stood with their arms folded smiling smugly to each other. As they discreetly made their way up the street towards the car, the armed response unit had blocked them in. Mikey's first thought was to look for another getaway when the response unit's horn sounded and the boys looked in shock to see Paul's wide eyes and cheeky grin staring at them from behind the steering wheel. The boys all climbed in and Paul reversed back up the street.

"Where's Matty and Harvey?" Paul asked.

"They're gone" Mikey said.

"Gone, what do you mean they're gone?"

Mikey looked around at the others.

"They're just gone. Okay" Ronnie said softly.

"Oh, oh" Paul said loudly.

"What is it?" Mikey asked.

"Up ahead. Look."

Not far in front of them was a road block and Paul started to slow down.

"What are you doing?"

"Away to turn around, we'll have to find another way out."

"Put the foot down."

"But..."

Mikey started to push and fiddle around with the buttons and switches until the blue lights started to flash.

"Go for it" Mikey shouted.

Paul smiled and slammed his foot on the accelerator. As the van sped up, the two patrol cars that were blocking the road began to separate. Paul stared ahead and concentrated on the gap. He missed each car by inches on either side. The boys howled and gestured as they looked back at the police who were oblivious to who had driven through their road block.

The two armed men, who took Harvey as their hostage, managed to escape back to their car. The police marksmen, unable to obtain a clean shot, made an attempt to continue their pursuit but had to scramble to various patrol cars when a search for their own police vehicle was unsuccessful. The hunt for the armed men ended several miles from the scene as their car ran out of petrol. Realising they were surrounded by police marksmen, the two men dropped their weapons and lay on the floor. Harvey was arrested along with the men as he was mistaken for one of the wanted gang.

The boys laughed as they listened to the police radio with the news about the arrests but their smiles soon dropped from their faces when it was announced that one of the gang was pronounced dead at the scene while another unidentified male was also shot.

"Guys, what the hell happened back there?" Paul asked.

"Harvey set us up" Ronnie answered.

"How do you know that?"

"I saw him making a phone call at the take-away place when he went in to buy our food" Mikey said.

"So they're just going to shoot us now" Robbo commented.

"I don't think those guys that shot Matty had any-thing to do with Frank or Bruce."

"I wonder who else was shot" Alonso said.

A message came over the police radio from Smith who had been informed about the boys' getaway. He appealed to the boys that if they were listening, to get in touch with him immediately.

"Is anyone going to answer that?" Alonso said.

"I'm not, unless you want to say hello" Mikey offered Alonso the receiver.

Ronnie reached over and grabbed it out of Mikey's hand. He pulled it towards him and stretched the cord to its limit.

"I didn't murder my uncle."

The rest of the boys sit in silence and Paul pulled over to the side of the road.

"Keep driving Paul. I think they can maybe track us if we stop" Mikey said.

"Would this be Ronnie I'm talking to?" Smith asked.

"I'm not talking to you. I'm telling you. It was self-defence. He picked up the knife and tried to stab me. We struggled and fell to the floor. When I got up the knife was in him. Check the finger prints on the handle. I didn't even touch it."

"I'll do that Ronnie. In the meantime why don't you boys meet me and we can talk about this. I could come and meet you on my own. One of your friends is already dead. We don't want any more of you boys hurt…"

Ronnie let the receiver go and it sprung back towards the radio.

"Just turn it off" Ronnie mumbled.

Smith was half way through another little speech to the boys when Mikey switched it off.

Chapter 19

Although Billy appeared calm while he listened to the scanner about the armed men's failed attempt at capturing the boys, his palms had been sweating constantly. He sat with Kevin and another two acquaintances in the back of the pub waiting for an opportunity to help the boys without putting themselves at risk. With Billy's friends connections the two armed men would not last long in prison and within a day they would be pleading to be placed in solitary. They had already discussed the possibility of going after The Program's wardens to find out the truth about what happened, but at the moment, it was deemed a high risk.

Information had come through that the boys had dumped the van in a car park on the edge of the city but by the time Kevin had driven Billy to the area, it was swarming with blue lights. Billy knew that the boys would have been long gone, but he was insistent and wanted to be on hand if the police had picked up a tail. A message was put over the scanner to Smith that a police issue gun was missing from its casing. There was no reply from Smith.

Driving away from the scene, Kevin received a message on his pager. He pulled over at the nearest phone box and made a call. He received information that there had been a raid on Billy's fake hideout. He got back in the car and gave Billy the news.

"If this was a planned raid, why was it not on the scanner?" Kevin said.

"Smith is smarter than you think. He'll have used a different frequency. He knows we are listening. That's why he's not bothered about us hearing the information about the boys, he wants us to know, and he's waiting on me turning up" Billy said.

***

After dumping the police van, Paul walked ahead of the other boys in search of another form of transport. Ronnie kept talking about Matty being shot and killed, and as much as the rest of the boys felt bad for what happened, Ronnie was making it worse.

"But I mean that could have easily been any one of us."

"Look Ronnie, we know. Will you please stop going on about it" Robbo said.

"The thing is guys, if that's what the rest of us are looking at, then there's something I have to do."

"What? Oh don't tell me you're still a virgin Ronnie?"

"No. It's nothing to do with that."

"Well what is it? Spit it out."

"Mikey" Ronnie looked at him with pleading eyes.

Mikey knew what and who, was on Ronnie's mind."

"Ronnie I promise we'll go and see her tomorrow, but right now, if Paul hurries up and finds us a car, then I may have a good place for us to hide out tonight."

"Where" Paul asked

"Just get us a car" Mikey demanded.

It took Paul several attempts to break the steering lock on a fairly new car and the boys were soon mobile once again.

"So who is this person you want to go and see Ronnie?" Alonso asked.

"It's just someone I know. I need to thank her for what she did for me and the way things are going for us, probably goodbye."

"Don't say that Ronnie. It's going to work out."

Mikey directed Paul onto the dual carriageway and instructed him to turn off when he saw a familiar name on a sign post. Brian had taken him here not long after he had joined The Program and promised Mikey he would let him visit as often as possible. There was a small car park to the rear of the building, out of sight from passers-by.

"So what is this place?" Alonso asked.

"It's sheltered housing. My old foster mother lives here, we'll be safe for tonight."

"But I thought you hated your foster family."

"It's a different one. Come on let's go."

Mikey put the safety catch on the gun and put it down the front of his trousers. He crept quietly into the building with the boys close behind him. After knocking lightly on her door a low voice answered.

"Who is it?"

"It's me. It's Mikey."

The door opened and Anna looked out at the faces of the five boys. The looked tired and in need of a good scrub.

"Hurry up, come in before someone sees you" Anna said.

The boy's all nodded at Anna in acknowledgment as they entered her home. Ronnie went straight to the T.V. and sat down. The rest of the boys followed.

"I take it you boys are hungry."

They all nodded at Anna.

"Well get yourselves cleaned up and I'll make you something to eat."

"Thanks you" They all said in turn.

Mikey followed Anna into the kitchen to give her a hand and shut the door behind him.

"We didn't do it Anna."

Anna looked up at Mikey and stroked his face.

"I know son."

Mikey saw tears in her eyes and hugged her gently. For a few seconds his mind was transported back to when he was a small boy and he was safe in her and Charlie's company. Ronnie knocked on the kitchen door and as he entered, they released their embrace and Anna wiped her eyes.

"I was just wondering if you needed any help."

"No. It's okay Ronnie we'll be fine."

Ronnie went back into the living room and joined the other boys who were sitting eagerly around the T.V. waiting on the news to come on. Anna served up the boys some hot soup and watched with a smile as they devoured a whole loaf of bread between them. Later as they tucked into a plate of sausage, chips and beans the news eventually come on. The reporter confirmed that one of the gang had been shot and killed by vigilantes who were out to collect the reward money. One of the Security Wardens Bruce Harrington from The Program had also been shot and was in intensive care in Ninewells hospital under police guard. The reporter also went on to say that two men have been arrested after a police chase. They believed that they had taken one of the gang as hostage until their getaway car ran out of petrol. The boys saw the funny side of this and even Anna broke into a smile.

"Traitor" Robbo shouted, when Harvey's face was shown on the screen.

"...although Graham Harvey was a former resident of The Program, he was not a member of the wanted gang. However, he has been arrested on suspicion of aiding and abetting the gang after their brutal murder of Brian Malliff. Due to the involvement of firearms, the police have now stepped up their search and deployed armed officers to various parts of the city."

Ronnie reached over and changed the channel "I hate the way they portray us to be a gang."

"What do you think we should do Anna?" Mikey asked.

"Well, the last thing I want is for any of you boys to get hurt. I could get in touch with one of Charlie's old friends. His son is a long distance lorry driver. He could maybe take you somewhere."

The boys didn't answer. They were in deep thought contemplating their options.

"Thanks Anna, we'll have a think about it" Mikey said.

"You boys had best get some rest. There are spare blankets and pillows in the cupboard in the hall. You will have to make room on the floor."

"That's okay Anna. It's probably one of the more comfy places we've had to sleep in a while" Mikey said.

"Good night boys."

"Good night Anna." The boys said before she disappears into her bedroom.

"So what do you think Mikey? Do you think we should maybe take off someplace else for a while?" Robbo said.

"And let Frank and Bruce go free after what they did to Brian."

"Mikey we're not going to get near them now. Bruce has guards around his hospital room you heard it yourself. Not to mention the armed police all over the city who I'll bet are just waiting for the chance to take us out. I think we should consider it."

"For once I think we agree on something" Alonso said.

"Well I'm staying. I'm going to stay until the job is done" Mikey said.

"Why Mikey? You know anything you do is not going to bring Brian back."

"Look guys. Before Brian put me on The Program I had nothing. My life was destined to be spent locked up. We could take a chance and go live somewhere else, but what if we get caught, then all of this will be for nothing. You know we have to finish it for Brian...and Matty. I'm staying and I'm going to see it through."

"Me too" Paul said.

"Me too, but I have something I need to do first" Ronnie nodded at Mikey.

"We'll go in the morning Ronnie. What about you two?"

Alonso looked at Robbo and back to Mikey. You're right. We should see it through for Brian."

All the boys looked at Robbo and he smiled. "We'll see it through" He nodded.

Alonso thought he had woken first until he heard someone in the bathroom. He looked around the floor. It must be Ronnie he thought. He went into the kitchen and poured himself a glass of water. On his return the bathroom door opened and Anna appeared. Alonso stood in the doorway confused.

"Are you okay?" Anna asked.

"Eh, yeah, I thought it was Ronnie in the toilet, that's all."

The two voices woke the others up.

"What's wrong?" Mikey asked.

"I'm just wondering where Ronnie is?"

"What do you mean?"

"Well. He's not here"

"Are you sure?"

"Mikey. He's gone."

"But why would he leave? Where would he go?" Anna asked.

"I have a pretty good idea. What time is it?"

"Near half past eight, why?"

"Come on guys. We need to hurry."

"Where to"

"I'll tell you on the way. Let's go."

The boys quickly said their goodbyes to Anna and thanked her for letting them stay. They hurried to the car and drove in the direction of Leslie-Ann's school. Paul drove slowly up and down the narrow streets surrounding the school as they searched frantically for Ronnie.

"What will we do if we can't find him?" Alonso asked.

"Go back to Anna's and wait for him there I guess."

"Wait. I think I saw him. Stop" Robbo said.

"Where" Paul asked

"Over there by the trees, just up from the main gate."

"What is he doing?"

"Nothing, he's just standing there."

"He's waiting on Leslie-Ann" Mikey said.

"What do we do? If we go and get him we'll all be seen."

"Paul, pull over and park on the pavement off the main road and keep it running. We'll wait here and see what happens."

The boys watched Ronnie from a short distance. He stood by the trees impatiently while he inspected every car that pulled up. The bell sounded and Ronnie was about to give up hope when a car pulled up close to the entrance. A small red haired girl stepped out and Ronnie's eyes lit up. He tried to stay calm and waited until her father drove off but she was about to enter the school and he knew this was his only chance.

"Leslie-Ann" He shouted in a low voice.

She kept walking.

"Leslie-Ann" He shouted louder.

She turned her head to see a tall dark figure hiding in the trees. She knew his voice and without thinking she ran to him."

"No, go back. Your dad will see me."

She ignored him and kept running. She dropped her schoolbag on the ground and threw her arms around him.

"I missed you Ronnie."

"I only came to explain. I didn't want you to think..."

"It's okay. I know you would never do that."

Ronnie smiled to himself as he draped his arms around her. His moment of happiness was cut short as Leslie-Ann's father grabbed him from behind and tackled him to the ground. Ronnie didn't resist and kept his eyes on Lesley-Ann. Mikey, Robbo and Alonso ran to help him. Ronnie was now on his feet with both arms locked behind his back. Leslie-Ann was crying and shouting at her father to let him go but Ronnie reassured her that it was going to be okay.

"Dad, please don't do this" She pleaded with her father.

"Let him go" Mikey shouted.

Leslie-Ann's father turned to face the other boys and Mikey lifted up his shirt to reveal the gun. He took it out and pointed it in the direction of Lesley-Ann's father. Mikey had no intension of using it but hoped it would scare him into letting Ronnie go.

"Now son, don't you do anything stupid with that."

"Mikey, put the gun down. He's only protecting his daughter. Any good father would do the same. Please Mikey, put the gun down."

Mikey took a step towards them and lifted the gun closer to his head.

"Let him go."

Lesley-Ann's father released Ronnie and backed away. Mikey lowered the gun.

During the commotion other teachers and parents had been alerted and were running towards them.

"Come on Ronnie, we need to go" Mikey said.

Ronnie turned to face Lesley-Ann's father.

"I'm not leaving Mikey. You go. I'm going to stay here. I'm ready to face them and tell the truth."

"Ronnie, come on, we have got to go" Mikey shouted.

"I never killed anybody" Ronnie said, while still look-ing at Lesley-Ann's father.

Lesley-Ann wrapped her arms around him tightly. Her father saw his daughter's pleading eyes and seen that the other teachers were closing in on them.

"I think you had better go now, before they get here" Her father nodded towards the approaching teachers.

"Thanks" Ronnie said. Her father gave him a satisfied nod.

He kissed Leslie-Ann on the forehead and turned to face the other boys.

Before they ran off, Mikey held the gun up again. "The safety was on" He said as he smiled at Lesley-Ann's father.

The teachers and parents stopped running when they reach Leslie-Ann and her father.

"Did they hurt you?" One of them asked.

"No. We're fine" Leslie-Ann looked at her father and they both smiled.

"What the hell are you playing at Ronnie? You could have got us all caught" Robbo said.

Ronnie didn't answer. He sat in the back of the car with a satisfied smile.

Chapter 20

Anna heard a sharp knock on the door and immediately pictured the police waiting to question her. She opened the door to someone who appeared to be familiar but couldn't quite place him.

"Hello Anna" The stranger said with fond smile.

As soon as he spoke she realised who he was.

"Billy."

He stepped towards her and they both hugged.

"What in the hell happened Anna?"

"I think you had better come in and sit down."

Billy followed Anna inside and closed the door.

"By the way, you've just missed Mikey. He stayed here last night with his friends."

***

The boys decided to go back to the crematorium as they felt that they never had the chance to say a proper goodbye to Brian. Apart from some old lady walking around, the place was empty. The police and reporters would be busy taking down the fabricated details of what happened at Lesley-Ann's school.

Brian's urn had been temporarily placed next to a small plaque on the grass and the boys sat down in a semi-circle and stared at it.

"It's not what I was expecting" Alonso said.

"Me neither" Said Mikey.

"That's so sad, after everything he did for other people. You would think they would have given him a suitable headstone."

"You don't get headstones when you get cremated."

"Why?"

"I don't know. I think some people bury the ashes with other relatives who are already buried."

"What do you think Brian would say if he saw us here right now?" Ronnie asked.

"He would probably tell us to hand ourselves in." Paul said.

"Maybe, but he wouldn't want us to be convicted for his murder. I don't think he would want Frank getting away with it either. No, I think he would be proud of us for sticking together and getting as far as we have" Mikey said.

Ronnie nodded "I think he would be proud of us."

"So what's the plan now? What's next?" Alonso asked.

There was a long silence.

"I think we should finish it" Ronnie said.

"What do you mean?" Alonso asked.

"You know what I'm saying. We need to go after Frank. He can't get away with this. We need to do this for Brian."

Mikey smiled. He took the gun out of his waist band and held it out in front of Brian's urn "For Brian."

Ronnie placed his hand on top of Mikey's "For Brian."

Paul did the same, then Robbo. The rest of the boys looked at Alonso. He stared at the plaque for a few seconds and then back to the boys. "For Brian" He said, before gently slapping his hand on top of the others.

"I think we should all make a promise, that from now, if anything happens to any one of us, the others have to continue to go after Frank and Bruce or anyone else responsible for Brian's death" Mikey said.

The boys all made their promise.

***

Billy said a tearful goodbye to Anna and promised her that he would keep in touch. He had another important house visit to make and Kevin had been busy listening intently to the police scanner to make sure the roads were clear ahead. It also updated him on the recent activity of the boys.

The house was located in a respectable area with tidy gardens and expensive cars parked outside. Billy walked up the path to the front door and was about to knock but after trying the door and finding it open, he decided to walk in and catch them off guard. The hallway was immaculate and smelled like a hospital. He peered into the living room where a large man was sat in a chair reading his paper. Billy casually walked in and sat opposite.

"What the...?"

"Shh" Billy put his finger to his lips "Do you know who I am?"

"I have no idea" The man said smugly.

The man moved his newspaper to the side and Billy clocked his massive gut. Billy stood up quickly and in a downward motion he punched his fist into the man's gut. The man bolted upright in his seat and clutched his stomach. He coughed and spluttered while Billy casually sat back down opposite.

"Just so that I know I have the right person. I'm going to ask you again. Do you know who I am?"

The man looked up with a face of agony and nodded.

"Good. That will save me the trouble in explaining why I'm here. I take it you are Harry?"

Billy nodded and stared until Harry nodded back. Billy then pulled out a neatly folded rag from his pocket that Kevin had handed him only minutes before and placed it on his lap. He slowly started to unfold the rag to reveal a small handgun.

"Look. I never meant Mikey any harm. We took good care of him. You know how boys are. He was a bit of a handful, so we had to be strict with him."

"Strict with him" Billy made a face before he lunged forward from his seat to smack Harry in the side of the head with the gun.

"Now, what did you do with those letters?"

"What letters?"

Billy lunged forward and took a harder swing with the handgun. Harry cried out and clutched his head. Billy casually sat back down and watched the blood trickle down Harry's face.

"I'm going to ask you again. What did you do with the letters?"

"I don't know what letters you're talking about" Harry was crying.

Billy stood up. He was about to unleash serious damage on Harry when he heard footsteps approaching. The living room door opened and as Linda entered, Billy pointed the gun at her.

"Here" In her hand was a small pile of envelopes.

Billy recognised his hand writing. He took them from her and placed them inside his jacket pocket. He leaned over Harry and smashed him several times with the gun. Linda screamed and tried to stop him but Billy pushed her away. When Billy was finished, Harry was slouched in his chair and his blood had spayed up the wall. Linda was on the floor crying.

Billy got back in the car and took the rag out of his pocket. He started cleaning the blood from the gun before wrapping it back up.

"Why didn't you use the gun?"

"I did" Billy smiled, he knew what Kevin meant.

Kevin smiled and drove off.

***

Smith received an urgent call by Nevin concerning a serious assault in a house on the edge of the city. When he arrived on the scene, a large man whose face was unrecognisable was being assisted into an ambulance.

"You're not going to believe this one" Nevin said.

"The boys didn't do this, surely."

"No, it was an older brother of one of the boys, someone that you used to be well acquainted with."

"Billy McDonnell" Smith replied. "And who are they?" He nodded towards the couple in the ambulance.

"Michael's old foster parents, the statement from the mother said Billy came looking for some letters that he had sent to his brother over the years. Apparently the parents never passed them on to him."

"He's not seen his brother in over ten years. They obviously lost touch when Michael was with them and now he's looking for the letters to prove that he tried to keep in contact. Billy must be getting ready to make a move to help them. I have an idea, come on. We have to move."

***

Mikey's plan was to go back to Anna's and hide out until dark but on approaching the sheltered housing complex they spotted officers in an unmarked police car, not too far from the main entrance.

"So what do we do now?" Paul asked.

"I don't know. Just drive" Mikey said.

"Where to"

"I don't know, anywhere. Just drive until we can think of someplace to go."

"That's not a good idea Mikey. There is police everywhere and this car has probably been reported stolen by now"

"Paul's right Mikey, we need to hide out until tonight" Ronnie said.

"I think I know a place" Alonso said.

"I hope it's not one of those churches where you have to take off your shoes, kneel down and pray to some God is it?" Robbo said.

"That's called a mosque and no it's not there."

"I don't care what it's called. If it's warm and safe then I'm up for it" Ronnie said.

"You'll need to give me directions Alonso" Paul said.

"You guys are not serious. I'm not going to some Paki mosque" Robbo said.

"If you have any other suggestions Robbo, then let us hear them. Like Ronnie said, if it's safe and warm, let's do it" Mikey said.

"Robbo, I don't go to a mosque and I'm not a bloody Paki, I'm Chilean."

"Whatever."

"Why haven't you mentioned this place before Alonso?" Ronnie asked.

"I never really thought about it. Remember my family hasn't spoken to me since I was sent to the Institution."

"Then who was it that came to visit you all those times?"

"That was Cristian, my oldest brother. My family didn't know he came to visit me or he would have been cut off from the family the same as me."

Alonso directed Paul to the Broughty Ferry area of Dundee. It was a rich area with large houses and surrounding walls and some had long winding driveways.

"Wow look at the size of those houses, they're like castles or are they hotels?" Ronnie asked.

"They're houses. Pull up here Paul. You guys wait here while I go and check it out."

Alonso walked down the street until he reached the surrounding wall at the rear of his house. When he looked up he thought about his family and longed for the days when they were all close. He pulled on the back gate but it was locked. He climbed over and kept to the far wall and walked behind the trees until he reached the families outhouse. The door to the outhouse was also locked but he felt along the back window ledge and found the spare key. It was always kept in the same place. He opened the door and felt around for the light switch. He looked around the room. Nothing had changed since he left for The Program. There were comfy chairs along the back wall and a table in the middle of the room. On the edge of the table was an envelope with Alonso's name written on it in large graffiti style writing. He knew the style. It was his brothers. He stepped into the room and tore it open.

"Hey Alonso, if you are reading this I guess you've not been caught yet and you're obviously running out of places to go. I know the family has washed their hands of you. Even more so now, but we (you're brothers) know you're not capable of murder. We have managed to scrape together some money (without Dad knowing) and have arranged transport back to Chile where you will be looked after and have a fresh start in life. There is a contact number for you to call and they will sort you out with a fake passport and go over the fine details. Take care and we will come visit you once you're settled."

Alonso sat down and stared at the letter. He knew his brothers must have gone to a lot of trouble to do this for him and it must have been hard to keep it all from his father. He felt torn between his friends and his family and knew the time was coming to make a decision that was best for him. He walked back to the car and told the others to follow him.

"This place is cool Alonso, what is it?" Mikey asked.

"It's sort of like an outhouse, me and my friends used to hang out here in the summer."

Mikey took the gun out of his trousers and put it on the coffee table. The rest of the boys stared at it. Paul picked it up and started aiming it around the room pretending to shoot random objects.

"If we get the chance can I shoot Frank?"

"You can shoot both of them if you want" Mikey said.

Paul smiled

"What about me I want to shoot one of them" Robbo said taking the gun from Paul.

"Guys, we are on the run for murder, we are trying to prove that we are innocent and all you are thinking about is who gets to kill who" Alonso said.

Paul and Robbo look at each other and smiled before they both said "Yeah"

Alonso stared at the two of them and watched intently as they passed the gun between them. He had visions of being shot and tried to imagine what it would feel like. He only relaxed once the gun was placed back onto the coffee table. The boys stretched out on the comfy chairs and it wasn't long before their tired eyes quickly drifted off to sleep.

Upon wakening only a few hours later Mikey notice Alonso was gone. He got up out of the chair and looked outside.

"Alonso" He said softly. There was no answer.

"Mikey I think you should see this."

Mikey took the letter from Ronnie and read it. "He's gone?"

Ronnie nodded.

"What do you mean he's gone?" Robbo said.

"It says something about a number to call."

"He's torn it off and left the note so that we know he's not coming back."

"Great. So what do we do now Mikey?" Ronnie asked.

"We do what we set out to do. We made a promise remember."

Mikey picked up the gun and put it back in his waist band.

"You guys ready?"

The boys nodded.

Chapter 21

Alonso had to call the number several times before someone answered. The person on the other end asked his whereabouts and told him to wait there and that someone would pick him up. Alonso was still unsure if what he was doing was the right thing. He walked away from the phone box and returned several times. In the end he decided to stay.

He was taken to a warehouse full of pallets of grocery supplies and was led into an office out the back. His oldest brother Cristian was waiting. Without saying a word they both hugged each other.

"It's good to see you Alonso."

They sat down and talked for a while and Alonso explained what really happened to Brian.

"So where are the rest of your friends?"

"I don't know. I left them in our outhouse. Their plan is to go after Frank and Bruce. Mikey has a gun."

"Alonso, don't get mad, but there is someone that needs to talk to you."

"Who is it?"

"He's a detective, but he's okay. It's him that has helped me arrange your escape. But he needs some information from you."

"Like what?"

Alonso's brother left the room and returned moments later with Smith. Alonso stood up and backed away from him.

"Calm down Alonso. I'm not here to arrest you. Please, sit down."

Alonso stood standing.

"Sit down." Smith demanded.

"Come on Alonso. Just sit down and talk to the detective then we can get you out of here."

Alonso reluctantly sat down opposite Smith who had his notebook ready.

"Right, where are the rest of the boys?"

"I left them sleeping at our outhouse. I don't know if they are still there."

"Where are they planning on going?"

Alonso clammed up. Smith knew they would be heading for Frank but he was trying to get Alonso talking to find out what he really wanted to know.

"Did you or any of the other boys take a gun from the police van that you used as a getaway?"

"Alonso shook his head."

"Look Alonso. If you care about your friends you need to tell me what I need to know. I want to help them."

Alonso nodded.

"Who took it?"

"Mikey."

"Does he still have it?"

Alonso nodded again.

"What is he planning on doing with it?"

Alonso shrugged.

"Is he going after Frank?"

Alonso shrugged again.

"Alonso, you need to help me so that I can help your friends and keep them safe."

"They're going after Frank and Bruce to make them confess to killing Brian."

"Well going after Bruce may be a waste of time, as I don't think he's going to make it anyway."

"Good." Alonso said.

"What about Scott? Who killed him?"

"He was already dead when we got there. I swear we only went there to ask him for help."

"It's okay. I believe you."

"Well if you believe me. Why haven't you arrested them then?"

"Has Mikey had any contact with his brother Billy?"

"No. Why? What does he have to do with any of this?"

"We just need to talk to him. We have information that he has entered into the country. Are you sure Mikey has had no contact with him?"

"I'm sure."

"What about any of Billy's friends? Have they contacted or tried to contact Mikey?"

Alonso shook his head.

Smith put his notepad away.

"So are you going to arrest Frank and Bruce?"

"Eventually, but right now we need them as bait for Mikey and we need Mikey as bait for his brother." Smith said with a smug grin on his face.

He got up to leave and turned back. "Oh and I hope you have a safe journey back to Chile." He was still grinning.

Alonso's brother gave him the thumbs up and smiled but Alonso did not share his enthusiasm. He sat in silence as it sunk in that Smith had been using him and the rest of the boys to try and capture Mikey's brother. Once they have him, they would go 'all out' to catch his friends. Now that Alonso had confirmed to him that Mikey was armed, they would shoot to kill. It also made him realise that if Smith could go to those lengths to catch Mikey's brother, there was no way he was ever going to let him leave. He had to get back to the boys and warn Mikey that the whole thing was a trap.

***

Billy and his friends had been waiting patiently on the news when a message came over the police scanner. It was a possible address of where the boys could be heading. It also warned officers not to approach them under any circumstances as it had now been confirmed they were in possession of a police firearm.

"It's time to make our move Billy" Kevin said.

"Okay call the grass. Let him know what's happening. Tell him to stay there and we will pick him up on the way. That should give him enough time to inform Smith."

Billy picked up the shotgun from the table and started to load it. There was another automatic gun still on the table and Kevin took out a small box of rounds and began to load it.

"Are those blanks?" Billy asked.

"Sure are. This weapon is for our little talkative friend" Kevin smiled.

After the grass received the phone call, he hung up and dialled Smith's number.

"Smith"

"This is D.C.I Smith."

"Billy is about to make his move."

"This had better be for real. You're skating on thin ice after that hideout fiasco."

"It's real." He hung up. 'Skating on thin ice' 'Fiasco' I think he's watched too many detective movies. He thought.

***

A car pulled up several streets away and the po-lice surveillance called over the radio to confirm it was the boys. Smith only had to give the order and those boys would be in custody in a matter of minutes but he hesitated. He wanted Billy.

"Chief Inspector, our men can take them now while they are all together, if we let them go any further Frank's life could be at risk" Nevin said.

"They are not altogether. There is more to come."

"What do you mean?"

"I have information that Billy McDonnell is also heading this way."

"Excuse me Chief, but our job is to make sure that those boys or anyone else for that matter do not come to any harm."

"Excuse me Detective, but it's Chief Inspector and I give the orders here."

"But Sir...?"

"We wait." He snapped.

"Fine, but if this goes wrong, it's on you."

Smith shrugged his shoulders and looked back out onto the street.

Mikey checked the gun before leaving the car. He took the safety catch off and put it in his waistband. The four boys walked nervously down the street towards Frank's house, unaware they were being watched from every angle.

"Which way" Robbo asked.

"What do you mean?"

"Back or front?"

Mikey thought for a second.

"The front, we're going straight through the front door. It's time to finish this once and for all."

Mikey's enthusiasm gave Robbo a lift in his step and Paul an extra inch on his swagger. They reached Frank's gate and looked up the path to his door. Mikey took the gun out of his waistband and turned to the others. "You guys ready?"

The boys nodded.

Mikey looked at Ronnie and they both faced the door and charged towards it. Both of their shoulders hit the door hard and the lock loosened. Ronnie gave it another hard kick and the door swung open. They entered the living room to find Frank getting to his feet.

"What the...?"

"Hello Frank" Mikey smiled as he pointed the gun at him.

Frank put his hands out in a calming motion "Mikey, don't do anything stupid."

"Get on your knees."

Frank took a step forward and Mikey clicked back the leaver.

"Knees, now" Mikey demanded.

Frank dropped to his knees and Mikey lifted the gun to his temple.

A loud crash was heard from the back door and five armed men with ski-masks come rushing through the house.

"Don't do it Mikey" A familiar voice said.

The boys froze.

"Mikey it's me, it's Billy."

Mikey lowered the gun.

"What...W...?"

Smith put the loud speaker to his mouth. "This is Detective Chief Inspector Smith. The house is completely surrounded. Put your weapons down and come out with your hands in the air."

Mikey stood in shock. "Billy...What...?"

"We'll talk later Mikey. Right now, we need to go."

Mikey looked at Billy and then turned back to Frank. He lifted the gun and placed against Frank's head.

"Mikey, don't do it. If you do that, you will become exactly what they've said you are, a murderer."

"What's the difference? They're never going to believe us anyway."

Through the window, a sharp shooter informed Smith that he had one of the suspects in his sights. As Smith gave the signal to fire, Billy caught sight of the red dot on Mikey and quickly pushed him out of the way. The shot caught Mikey on the shoulder and he fell to the floor, the gun landed close to Frank.

"We don't want anyone else hurt. Please drop your weapons and come out with your hands in the air." Smith announced over the speaker.

Frank looked down to the floor and clocked the gun. Billy, who was busy applying pressure to Mikey's wound, shouted at Kevin to kill the lights. Frank made his move and slid the gun underneath him.

With the house now in darkness, Nevin quickly arranged the police vehicles so that their full beams were directed towards Frank's house to assist the sharp shooters.

Back in the room, Paul could see Frank's silhouette across the floor and once his eyes become accustomed to the dark, he saw him slowly raise his arm and point the gun at Mikey.

"Mikey" Paul shouted and dived forward to try to grab it. Frank turned before Paul managed to reach him and fired a shot. Paul put his hands to his stomach and stumbled to the floor.

"Paul" Ronnie dived across the floor to him.

Frank, still holding the gun, was distracted by one of the police vehicles full beam lights being switched on and turned to face the window. A sharp shooter took the shot and Frank's body hit to the floor.

Ronnie cradled Paul as he lay in agony holding his stomach.

"I don't want to die Ronnie" He cried.

"You're not going to die Paul."

"How bad is he?" Billy asked.

"He's losing a lot of blood."

Billy crawled across the floor and lifted up Paul's sweatshirt. He leaned up and grabbed a pillow from the sofa and took the cover off. He placed it on Paul's wound.

"Keep the pressure on this."

"Please, put your weapons down and come out with your hands up" Smith pleaded.

"Billy we have to get out of here" Kevin said.

"Okay. Guys make your way to the back door"

Billy crawled back over to help Mikey. Ronnie tried to move Paul but he was in too much pain.

"You will have to leave him. He'll be okay. They'll take him to the hospital" Billy said.

"Ronnie, don't leave me" Paul said.

"Look. You can't come with us. You're bleeding really badly. They'll take you to the hospital" Billy said.

"Please Ronnie. I can't go back to the institution. I can't go back there."

"Come on Ronnie" Robbo said.

"Ronnie, please" Paul pleaded.

Ronnie looked over at the guys and back at Paul. "Guys, just go. I'm going to stay here with Paul."

Mikey stopped crawling.

"Come on Mikey. Keep going" Billy shouted.

"I'm staying too."

"What? Mikey if you want to get out of here we have to go now" Billy shouted.

"If they don't go, I don't go."

Billy looked up at Kevin and his friends who were now close to the back door. "We'll go get them" They said.

They started to crawl back through the house when they heard a commotion from outside. A loud horn was sounding and people were shouting to get out of the way. Billy looked up to see a police van crashing through Frank's gates and straight through the front of the house. He lifted up his shotgun and pointed it at the driver.

"No don't shoot. It's Alonso" Robbo shouted.

"Did you hear that Paul? It's Alonso. He's came back for us. Come on, someone give me a hand" Ronnie shouted as he tried to lift Paul.

They opened the side door of the van and as every-one was getting in, Billy took over the driving. While reversing the van back out, they could hear shots being fired by the police.

"Kevin we need to get this thing turned around. Give them another target to shoot at."

"Like what?"

"Do you want me to spell it out?"

"Got you" Kevin grabbed Billy's shotgun and hurried to the back of the van. He opened the door and fired a few shots into the air making the police duck for cover. This gave them a few seconds to turn the van. Kevin and one of his friends grabbed a hold of the Grass. They kicked him out of the van into the middle of the road and as they went to shut the doors, the Grass pointed his gun full of blanks at Kevin and fired. Kevin laughed as he pulled the van doors closed.

"Let's go Billy" He shouted.

The Grass turned to face the police. "I work for Smi…" The sharpshooters saw the gun still in his hand and opened fire. His body was filled with bullets while Billy made their getaway up the street.

"I can't believe you came back for us" Robbo said before he hugged Alonso.

"Yeah, even Paki's keep their promise" Alonso winked.

"How did you manage to steal the van?" Mikey asked.

"I had a good teacher" Alonso looked over at Paul.

"Come on Paul. Hang in there mate" Ronnie held up his head.

The van ripped along the side streets and several patrol cars followed but kept their distance due to the occupants being armed. The van stopped when it reached a dead end.

"What do we do now?" Mikey said.

"Don't worry, I, unlike you, thought this through" Billy said.

Ronnie and Robbo placed each of Paul's arms over theirs and helped him out of the van. They followed Billy's friends through a gap in the wall to two waiting cars.

Smith was informed of their escape and shouted at one of his officers, furiously demanding that he resign for leaving the keys in the police van. The officer tied to plead his case.

"Do you know what? Don't resign. You're fired." He shouted at him as he walked away.

He turned to Nevin "Twice, twice, they have left with our vehicles. How stupid can they be to leave keys in a police van while pursuing suspects?"

"Have we any leads as to where they are heading?"

Smith stood for a few seconds until he calmed down.

"Well we know that one of them is seriously injured and he is going to need medical attention so there is a slight possibility they will be visiting a hospital soon. Also, there was an escape route planned for Alonso to get him to Chile. I have the details. You drive while I radio it in."

"What are you waiting on?"

"The keys"

Smith searched his pockets and then suddenly realised he had left them in the ignition.

"They're in the car" He mumbled.

Nevin put her hands on her hips and looked at him with her eyebrows raised "Really, so are you going to inform the officer that you fired or will I do it?"

Smith mumbled to himself before getting into the car.

Chapter 22

Kevin and one of his friends drove the two getaway cars to their newly acquired hideout. Kevin called an acquaintance and arranged for a Doctor to meet them there. The hideout was an old pool hall that closed down some time ago. It had been accustomed by Kevin's firm to store various stolen goods. Both Mikey and Paul lay on a table out the back. They were injected with strong painkillers be-fore the Doctor went to work on them. Mikey's bullet had enter his shoulder and exited out the back leaving a clean wound, he was soon stitched up and ready to go but Paul was not so lucky, the Doctor needed more time.

When Mikey appeared from the back room, Billy handed him the letters.

"What are they?"

"The letters I sent. I eh...picked them up from a friend of yours" He winked.

"Harry, you went to see Linda and Harry"

Billy smiled.

"How did you know...?"

"...I saw Anna" He said fondly.

The Doctor appeared from the room after an hour of working on Paul.

"So how is he?" Ronnie asked.

"There is nothing more I can do for him now. Even if he had gone straight to the hospital, there would have still been little chance of recovery. The bullet is in too far and he has lost so much blood that even with the correct equipment, I would be lucky to have reached it in time."

Everyone's head went down.

"How long does he have?" Ronnie asked.

"Maybe a couple of few hours"

The tears began to flow down Ronnie's face. He turned to face his friends and they all gathered around to comfort him.

Billy didn't want to interrupt the boy's moment but he knew they were on a time restraint.

"Guys, sorry to interrupt but we have a four hour journey ahead of us, we need to be at Liverpool docks by early morning. You have to make a decision about your friend. We can drop him near a hospital on the way. See if they can fix him up" Billy said.

"I think we should let Paul decide" Ronnie said.

Mikey looked at Ronnie and nodded at the door to the back room. Ronnie got up and walked through. Billy and Kevin discussed their options. Alonso mentioned his intended escape and how Smith had apparently set it up to let him go.

"Forget it. He wasn't letting you go anywhere" Kevin said.

"At least one thing, we know where Smith is right now."

The door of the back room opened and Paul was on his feet with his arm around Ronnie's shoulder.

"Guys he's coming with us" Ronnie said.

They all give Ronnie a strange look.

"It's okay guys. He knows he doesn't have long, but he would rather spend it with us."

"I'll call ahead and make alternative arrangements for you Alonso. There may be a few stops on the way but they'll get you there safely and you'll be well looked after."

Alonso nodded in acknowledgement before helping Ronnie with Paul. The doctor gave Paul another injection.

"This will keep you numb for a while."

The other boys looked on. They tried to put on a brave face but they all knew he wouldn't last through the night.

Two cars drove out of the hideout. The one in front contained two of Billy's friends up front and Alonso with his new found friend Robbo in the back. Kevin was driving the other car with Billy upfront. Paul was in the back with Mikey and Ronnie at either side of him. They reached the town centre and drove slowly along Riverside. On the approach to the airport, they could see the blue flashing lights of the police vehicles. There was a commotion outside among the reporters after they received a tip off about the possible escape by one of the gang.

"That's Smith's car" Kevin pointed out to the side at a car on the grass verge.

Smith and Nevin abandoned it in the rush to search the airport.

The boys looked out of the window at the unmarked car. Paul was becoming weaker by the minute and was struggling to stay conscious but made the effort to lift himself up to see it.

"How about you guys let me go out with a bang?" Paul said.

"What do you mean?" Mikey asked.

"I mean, find me a brick and a screwdriver. Come on guys, you know what I'm good at."

Mikey and Ronnie looked at each other and smiled.

"Billy, we need to make a stop" Mikey said.

"Are you guy's crazy? Have you seen the amount of police out there?"

Billy turned and looked back at his baby brother and his two friends.

Mikey turned to Paul "Are you sure you want to do this?"

Paul looked at Ronnie who had tears rolling down his face.

"Thanks for everything Ronnie" Paul said.

Billy instructed Kevin to turn back. He flashed his lights to the car in front and both cars stopped. Kevin signalled for them to follow him back to the airport. The police surrounding the airport were occupied in trying to contain the press and the two cars pulled up close to Smith's car unnoticed. While Ronnie and Mikey helped Paul to get out of the car, Robbo and Alonso came running over.

"What's going on?" Robbo asked.

None of the boys answered. Billy reached towards Paul and handed him a screwdriver and the others realised what was happening.

"You have a scanner too right" Paul nodded to Billy.

Billy smiled and shook his head. He passed Paul the scanner and left the boys to say their goodbyes.

"Thanks for everything Ronnie."

Ronnie wanted to say something but was too choked up. The tears rolled down his face and when he looked around, the rest of the boys were also crying.

"Hey come on guys, don't feel bad. We finished what we set out to do right?" Paul said.

He put hand out with his palm facing down.

Mikey wiped the tears from his face and placed his palm on top "We couldn't have done it without you."

Alonso reached forward and then Robbo.

Ronnie still had one arm around Paul holding him up. He looked around at the others and smiled before placing his palm on top of the others.

"Right guys, you best get out of here and let me do my thing. Oh and can you all do me a favour?" Paul asked.

"What's that?" Ronnie replied.

"Don't get caught."

Billy asked Kevin to ride with his two friends in the other car so that all the boys could travel together with him. Mikey got in the front with Billy, while Ronnie, Alonso and Robbo got in the back. Paul waited until the two cars were out of sight before he struggled towards Smith's car. His breathing was becoming shallower with each step. He reached Smith's car and lifted the scanner to smash the window but upon looking inside, he found the keys dangling from the ignition. He opened the door and winced in pain as he slowly moved himself behind the wheel. The injection the doctor gave him was wearing off. He reversed back out onto the main road but before he drove off, he picked up the control from the police radio and laid it on his lap.

"Hey Smith, I thought you would have learned by now, not to leave your keys in your car" Paul said over the police airwaves.

Smith looked at Nevin and they both started running out of the airport.

"All cars, all cars, the gang are mobile in an unmarked patrol car" Nevin shouted over the radio.

Smith called the headquarters to do a trace on his car. He ran to the nearest patrol car to give chase but it was blocked in by one of the reporters. The information came over the police radio from headquarters as they searched for the next available car. "Suspects are currently heading east along Riverside Drive."

"They are heading back into the city" Nevin said.

Smith shouted at an officer and demanded the keys to his patrol car. By the time they had a clear exit onto the main road; many other patrol cars were in front of them, pursuing Paul.

"Good one Paul" Billy said as a patrol car sped past them in the opposite direction.

Paul looked in the mirror to see the flashing lights behind him. He turned on the stereo and flicked through Smith's tapes.

"Hey Smith, you haven't got very good taste in music have you?" Paul said over the airwaves. He mentioned a few of the titles, much to Smith's embarrassment.

"It's okay, I've brought my own."

Paul took a tape out of his pocket and slammed it in the stereo. He kept the control button down so that the music broadcast over the police airwaves. The boys smiled at each other as they heard the rolling stones play back to them through the scanner.

"You know where he's heading don't you?" Ronnie said.

"Where" Billy asked

"The bridge"

"Come on Paul you can do it. Hang in there" Robbo shouted.

Paul sank further into the seat as he struggled to keep his eyes open. He put his foot down on the accelerator and sped up until he reached the slip road onto the bridge. As he turned on the bend he picked up the control to his mouth.

"Bye guys."

Paul held the button down as he raced towards the new temporary barrier. He ducked down as he crashed through it. The control dropped to the floor which cut off the music from the airwaves. The boys sat patiently listening to the officers as they gave chase. The car hit the side of the bridge and flipped over onto its roof and skidded along the road before coming to a stop. Billy turned off the scanner.

"Way to go Paul" Mikey said softly.

The boys sat in silence for most of the journey. Billy thought they were asleep until he looked at them staring out the windows into the darkness. It was the early hours of the morning when Billy arrived at Liverpool docks. He was met by an acquaintance from the ship who directed them to an old security office. It was a small heated room with comfortable chairs and coffee making facilities. They were instructed to stay there out of the way for a few hours until it was time to board. Kevin and his friends had planned on driving straight back to Dundee but decided to wait and see Billy off. The next few hours went by quickly for the boys as they were entertained by Kevin and Billy as they reminisced about some of their past adventures.

Alonso was informed that the ship he was boarding was leaving soon. He had another two connections until he would reach Chile but he was assured that he was in good hands. It was still dark when they emerged from the office to walk Alonso to his ship.

Mikey shook his hand "You have the address of my brother's place right?"

Alonso nodded and tapped his pocket. He turned to Robbo and offered him his hand. Robbo stepped forward and unexpectedly hugged him "I'll miss you mate. Where is it you're going again?"

"Chile. It's full of Paki's" Alonso winked.

"How long are you going for?" Robbo asked.

"Until things cool down, or until we hear word that we're in the clear. Why, are you thinking of visiting?"

Robbo nodded.

"You're welcome to come, all of you."

Alonso received a signal that he was clear to board.

"Guys please do as Paul asked. Don't get caught. I promise I will write once I get settled."

Alonso boarded the ship and the boys waved.

"Would you really visit Chile Robbo?"

Robbo nodded. "I would probably go now if I could."

They both turned to look at him.

"What. You really think I wouldn't go?"

"Well, you had better decide now, the ship is about to leave" Ronnie joked.

Robbo smiled at them and turned to face the ship. He turned to face them once again and his smile grew bigger. Without saying goodbye he turned and ran towards the ship. Mikey and Ronnie looked on in shock as he caught up with Alonso. A few words were exchanged and Alonso patted him on the shoulder. They both turned and waved.

"I wish the rest of the guys could be here to see this." Ronnie said.

"And Brian" Mikey added.

"Yeah definitely Brian" They both smiled.

Mikey and Ronnie got back to the office and the others laughed when Mikey explained about Robbo.

"I feel bad that I'm laughing. I feel like I should be grieving" Ronnie said.

"It's a long boring boat ride. You'll have plenty of time to grieve later" Billy said.

The sun was beginning to rise as they left the office and the temperature had dropped considerably. Kevin and his friends walked with them and Mikey and Ronnie looked on at their unemotional goodbye. It was as though they would see each other in the pub the next day. They boarded the ship and Ronnie mentioned that he kept expecting Smith to turn up any minute. The ship drifted slowly away from the dock and after making the final payment for their travel, Billy and the boys were shown to their accommodation. It was a tiny room with bunk beds and Mikey quickly jumped up to claim the top one as it had a porthole view. He lay back and watched as the dock appeared further and further away.
   "Hey Mikey, do you think Robbo will be alright with Alonso?"
   Mikey laughed at the thought of Robbo being in a foreign country with his racist attitude.
   "He'll be fine, Alonso will look after him."
   They both laughed again and nothing more was said between them as they drifted off to sleep.

Chapter 23

One year later

Mikey woke with the hot sun shining on his face through the gap in the curtain. Billy usually had to drag him out of bed for work in the morning, but not today. He was up before anyone else and headed straight for the kitchen. He sat on the balcony with his bowl of cereal and watched the large boats enter and leave the harbour down below. Mikey savoured every moment of his relaxing time as he knew it wouldn't be long until he was out in the hot baking sun, sanding and painting some of the smaller boats nearer the shore. Although he had turned sixteen recently and was old enough to leave and travel on his own, he liked it here and for the first time in a long time he was happy and felt settled. His thoughts drifted back to the many homes that he had in recent years and with each one, they brought something different into his life. He was soon distracted and brought back to reality by a noise in the kitchen. He knew it couldn't be Ronnie, as he was worse than him at getting up in the morning.

"Oh you're up. I was just about to wake you" Billy said looking out on to the balcony.

He poured himself some coffee and joined him.

"Why are you up so early?"

"I don't know, I just woke up" Mikey said in between slurps of milk and cereal.

"Well you'll be happy to hear that you'll only be working a half day today."

"Why is that?"

"I have to go and pick up some supplies."

"I thought they delivered them?"

"I need them now. I could wait days on them being delivered so it would be quicker to drive through and pick them up. Also, Nina wants to go shopping."

Although this is the main holiday resort on the island and contains the most bars and restaurants there are no hardware stores. The nearest is a long drive to the other side of the island. Mikey smiled at the thought of having the afternoon off and lounging around on the beach.

"You and Ronnie could come with us if you want."

"Nah, I think I'll stay here" The thought of waiting around on Nina going from shop to shop did not ap-peal to him. He finished his cereal and woke Ronnie with the good news. Mikey had never seen Ronnie move so quickly to get up for work.

They arrived at the boat shed, which was situated not far from the beach. Billy went into the office and made himself more coffee while Mikey and Ronnie opened the large wooden doors and pulled out the trailer containing the boat they had been working on. It had been booked in for small sanding job but due to the amount of layers of paint that had been applied over the years; the boys had been hard at it for days. Billy could have left the boys working on it while he was away for the day but he knew they deserved some time off. Ever since they arrived on the island Billy had them working nearly every day from early till late. Mikey was not stupid, he knew Billy was doing this to keep them busy and out of trouble. When they did have a day off it usually resulted in Billy taking them on a pub-crawl where they mingled with the holiday-makers. Ronnie, although he acted a bit slow sometimes, was certainly not slow when it comes to girls as he was always the first one over chatting to them. Billy usually sat back and left them to it. He paid their wages to them in cash and if they choose to spend it on some girl in one night then that was up to them. He was like that once himself and knew their way of thinking.

The boat the boys have been working on looked like a small toy next to some of the larger boats by the harbour. They wheeled the trailer out as far as the extension line would go so that they could work on the boat outside. The boys preferred jobs like this as they could watch what was going on around them while they worked. Later that morning when the beach filled up, strangers would walk by and sometimes stop for a chat. With all the attention they had not long ago, they were surprised that nobody ever recognised them. Mikey had grown his hair long since then and according to Ronnie, he looked more like a hippie surfer than a dangerous murderer that he had been labelled by the newspapers. Ronnie hadn't changed much though, to Mikey, he still looked the same from that first day when Brian introduced them. He was tall and dopey looking with scars from head to toe. Mikey also had many scars but his were psychological, the ones that were engraved in his mind that no one could see, the ones that he tried his hardest to forget.

Since they arrived on the island, Billy had talked about what happened and explained to Mikey that he was not much older than he was now when things went bad for him. He had got himself into so much trouble that he had no option but to leave or face doing a long spell in prison. Billy had gone to see Mikey before he left and knew that Charlie and Anna would take great care of him. If he knew that Mikey had been removed from Anna's care he would have made arrangements to come for him sooner.

Nina arrived with the sandwiches and cold juice for everyone and they all sit in the shade as they enjoyed the break from the sun.

"So what are you guys going to do today?" Billy asked.

"Hang out at the beach" Mikey said.

He looked over at Ronnie who nodded back.

"Yeah, well make sure you don't do anything stupid and get yourself into any trouble."

"Why do you always say that? We haven't been in trouble since we got here, well, except from that time when that man came looking for me because Ronnie got his daughter drunk" Mikey said.

"That was funny" Ronnie said.

"Maybe for you, but you weren't the one who had some crazy man running after you saying he was going to kill you."

"Look guys, I just don't want to come back and have the police at me. The next thing everyone will know who you are" Billy said.

Mikey knew why Billy was concerned. It would only take one stupid mistake, as the slightest hint of the wrong people knowing where they were, and their life here would over. They finished their sandwiches and got back to work. The rest of the morning went in quickly for the boys and it was soon time for them to pack up the tools. The beach was crowded now with holiday makers soaking up the rays from the sun and

Mikey stopped for a few seconds to take in the view. Ronnie nudged him and made a comment about some girl not too far from them.

"No need to guess what you two will be doing all day" Billy said.

He locked up the boat shed and Nina drove the boy's back to the apartment.

"We'll be back about six" Billy said.

The boys watched them drive off and went straight up to the apartment to get changed from their working clothes. They were back out minutes later with towels under their arms. As they walked down to the beach they passed the local shop and decided to buy some ice cream. Mikey also picked up a newspaper.

"Twentieth of the ninth, ninety, not bad, only a day old" Mikey said.

Ronnie raised his eyebrows. Mikey liked to catch up on what was happening back home but Ronnie refused to read them after all the lies they printed about him. Mikey didn't mind, in a way he kind of liked all the attention, even though sometimes the stories were wrong and quite hurtful. They made their way to their favourite place on the beach, a small sandy platform, where, even from lying down, they had a view of the beach.

"Why do you bother buying those?" Ronnie said as Mikey opened the newspaper.

"I just like to find out what's been going on back home."

"What? You don't consider this home?"

"Yeah of course, I mean, ah you know what I mean."

"Do you ever think about going back?"

"Sometimes, but I know it would only be to cause more trouble."

"Yeah me too, I still think about Leslie-Ann. I some-times wonder what she's doing right now and if she ever thinks about me."

"Of course she does"

"You think so?"

"Yeah, or course"

"I was about to call her a while back."

"Did you?"

"No, it would have been pointless really" He looked away.

"You did. Didn't you?"

Ronnie looked back with a cheeky grin.

"So what did she say?"

"She just asked how I was and stuff."

"Do you ever think about going back to see her?"

"Yeah all the time, but not just to see her, if I ever go back for another reason, it would be good to look her up to see how she was."

"I hope you didn't mention where we were."

"Come on Mikey, do I look that stupid?"

"Pretty much" Mikey laughed.

Ronnie dived on Mikey and they both wrestled for a few seconds.

"Ronnie, I don't get you mate. When any girls are around you are the first one over trying to chat them up, but here you are mopping about some girl you haven't seen in over a year"

"I know, but she was different, she meant a lot to me."

Mikey gave Ronnie a look and he was about to wrestle him again when a random girl in a bikini distracted him. She smiled at them as she walked by.

"I'll be back in a minute" Ronnie said as got up to follow her.

"See what I mean" Mikey shook his head and lay back with his newspaper.

He opened it up and smiled as he saw an old photo of himself staring back at him. There were photos of all the boys which accompanied another update of the on-going inquiry into the death of Brian.

'Ex Dundee Councillor Barney Williamson, charged with conspiracy to murder.'

Mikey wondered why they never printed a photo of the Councillor, but always seemed to print a whole page about the so called 'gang.' The story went on to say that the Councillor paid the two wardens who worked on The Program, extra bonuses to disrupt the boy's rehabilitation.

'It is now believed that the two wardens were tragically killed in circumstances that related to the boys' quest for retribution after the murder of their mentor, Brian Malliff'

Mikey looked at the photo of Brian and read on.

'A third warden from The Program, who it is now believed was murdered by the two, now deceased wardens, was the brother of Rosie Mitchell, who at the time of the murders, was Williamson's assistant. She is now a key witness against Williamson and will produce evidence to prove that he paid the two wardens to sabotage The Program. She will also

produce a notebook containing complaints that Malliff had recorded each time the wardens attacked the boys.'

Mikey had read most of this before and looked down the page to another paragraph that accompanied with the story.

'In a separate case against Williamson, a local businessman John Robertson, the father of one of the gang still at large, was giving evidence against Williamson in the scandal involving illegal contracts that were handed out to businesses linked to Williamson's company.'

Mikey looked at the photo of Robbo and smiled. They had received many letters from Chile and Alonso had said that he was happy in his new life but Robbo had been finding it difficult to settle. Mikey had suggested him coming to live with them but he had yet to hear back. At the foot of the page was a small photo of Smith, who after the 'gangs' escape, was forced into early retirement. He was also cited as a witness in the up and coming trial of Williamson.

"We never had a chance" Mikey mumbled to himself.

He closed the newspaper and threw it to the side. He now wished he had taken Ronnie's advice and not read it. He turned to lie on his stomach and caught sight of Ronnie splashing around in the water with the bikini girl. He closed his eyes and smiled as his mind drifted off to the first time that he met Ronnie, the same day he met Brian and the rest of the boys on The Program.

Printed in Great
Britain
by Amazon